Style Sisters

PARIS

PRINCESS

Liz Elwes

PICCADILLY PRESS • LONDON

To my parents – for everything.
To the fabulous writer Cathy Hopkins – whose amazing generosity
and kindness is legendary. I will be ever grateful.
To Giles Elwes and my children, William, Alice, Thomas and Jamie
for having such interesting lives and giving me so many lines
in the book (I hope you don't mind).
To my own style sisters: Frances Toynbee, Sarah Mower,
Jill Rothwell, Mary Saldanha, Marion Jeffrey, Anne Rands,
Rosie and Olivia McDonnell and Suzanne Vandevelde.
To Clare Elwes. To Johnny, Christine and Anne-Marie.
To Brenda Gardner, Ruth Williams, Melissa Patey and
everyone at Piccadilly for their help, patience and guidance.
To Bernice Green who started it.

First published in Great Britain in 2006
by Piccadilly Press Ltd.,
5 Castle Road, London NW1 8PR
www.piccadillypress.co.uk

A catalogue record for this book is available from the British Library

ISBN: 1 85340 879 4 (trade paperback)
ISBN-13: 978 185340 879 3

1 3 5 7 9 10 8 6 4 2

Printed and bound in Great Britain by Bookmarque Ltd
Cover design and text design by Simon Davis
Typeset by M Rules, London

Set in Fineprint, Kaufman and Stone Serif

Chapter 1

Tuesday 7.00 p.m.

'I just know I'm going to love her.'

'Carrie! You haven't even *met* her.'

'I *know*, but it's just a sort of spooky psychic feeling I have.'

'Bet you hate her.'

'Bet I won't.'

Rani sighed. 'You might. They might *all* be revolting. They might hate *us*. I bet they'll think we're pretty stylish though. What d'you think?'

I looked at her. She was sitting on my bedroom floor wearing a grubby T-shirt (mine), an old pair of pyjama bottoms (also mine) and a green face mask. She wasn't sleeping over; Rani just likes to make herself at home when she comes round.

'Hmm . . .' I said. 'I think I'm going to have to say, perhaps *not*.'

'But don't the French secretly envy our quirky English dress sense?'

Chloe raised her eyes from painting her toenails and looked Rani up and down. 'Absolutely, especially if by "quirky" you mean, ooh . . . completely and totally hideous.'

Rani's arm stretched under my bed for a slipper and threw it at her. She missed.

Chloe pulled a face but Rani was already distracted. She burrowed under my bed – she'd spotted my magazine stash when she found that slipper. 'Hey! Have you decided yet?'

I hung my head over the side of the bed, observing that half of

Rani had disappeared. 'Decided what?' I said to her legs.

'*What?* Ouch – I bumped my head! What do you think? What you are going to *wear*. *Je suis* trying to make sure we will be *très chic* and *belle. Pour les filles françaises.*'

'I didn't know they were Welsh.' Chloe waggled her toes to dry the varnish. For the dreamy, romantic type she can be quite sarcastic sometimes.

Beneath me, I heard the slither of a pile of mags collapsing.

'Ha very ha. Listen, you two; we've only got a few days to decide. And I feel it's vital we make a good impression from the *moment* they get off the coach.'

'I hear you,' I said solemnly.

'It's bad enough that a bunch of posh girls have had to come *here*, the middle of nowhere, without them being greeted by a wall of white trainers and velour tracksuit bottoms.'

'Oi, if you're referring to —'

There was a sigh from under the bed. 'No, I'm not talking about your mum, Carrie, though it *is* true that she has her own very individual and, er, distinctive style. I am talking about *us*. We need to dress to impress, so that they don't think that we are a bunch of bumpkins. Though seeing as the only social event they've got to look forward to is the welcome party at school on Monday night, there's every chance that's exactly what they'll think.' I could hear another page turn.

'So you're saying the pink-shell-suit-and-white-stilettos look I'd planned isn't going to work?' I went on.

There was a silence.

'Well, if you're going to take that attitude . . .'

'OK, OK, Rani, what are *you* going to wear?' Chloe was blowing on her toes now. Not easy.

Rani did a backwards wiggle and sat up, triumphantly clutching an article on eyebrow shaping. 'Well, since you're asking, I'm toying with either a casual jeans-and-boots look, topped with stripy T-shirt – to make them feel at home – or black mini, tights and baggy sweater for that "Paris student" look.'

'Brilliant, Rani, you've given me some ideas,' I enthused.

'Like what?'

'Dangling a couple of garlic cloves from my ears and shoving onions down my bra.'

'Well,' she said, tossing her shiny black hair over her shoulder (a lucky genetic legacy from her Indian dad), 'I won't say your frontage couldn't do with the help . . .'

'Can we not talk about frontage?' Chloe pleaded before I could respond. 'I want to talk about the French girls.'

Chloe never has to worry about frontage. She doesn't have to worry about any part of her anatomy. With her long, curly dark hair, green eyes and creamy skin she is naturally drop-dead stunning. Put her in a sad old T-shirt and PJ bottoms and she'd think of something stylish and original to do with them, so in the end you'd wish you were wearing them too. What with that and being a kind and thoughtful person it really is a wonder she has any friends at all.

'You're very confident that your exchange girl is going to be wonderful, Carrie.' She frowned. 'I mean, I'm sure she will be. I'm just hoping that they have a good time. And that *they* like *us*.'

'What's not to like?' I protested.

'French girls spend hours and hours on their appearance, you know,' said Rani. 'I bet we can learn things from them.'

'I know, like exercising,' I offered. 'I read that they never stop pointing and flexing their toned limbs.'

'Ooh, ooh,' Rani gasped. 'That reminds me. Look at this. I can teach them what my mum showed me from her yoga class. If you do this every day your bum will be as teeny-tiny as anything.' She threw herself forwards on to the floor. 'Look. You lie flat on your face like this. Then you slooooowy raise one leg behind you keeping it straight and pointy. Then the other one.'

'But, Rani, you don't have a big bum,' I protested.

'I know,' she panted. 'It's you and Chloe I'm thinking about.' And she collapsed sniggering into the carpet.

I walked across the room to get some more varnish and trod on her bum on the way over.

'Hey! That definitely comes under "What's Not to Like". You won't be making any new friends if that's the way you're going to behave. Violating people's personal space.'

The doorbell rang. 'That's my dad,' Rani said. 'We will have to continue our conversation tomorrow. But I am going to tell him that you trod on me on purpose.'

'Then I'll tell him that you want to snog Kenny and it is only the fact he is in bed with a bug that is keeping your lips apart . . .'

That did it. She shrieked, leaped up and ran around the room in a frenzy, pulling her uniform over the pyjama bottoms and T-shirt, stuffing the magazine (she did ask first) in her school bag and grabbing all her things together.

Rani's dad thinks all boys are predatory sex-maniacs. I also know that her dad had no idea of her future plans to plant her lips on Kenny's, because if he did, Kenny might see his health taking an even more dramatic downturn. She is hoping to see him tomorrow if his mum gives her permission to visit his sick bed. All visitors have been banned so far this week.

I, on the other hand, will *definitely* be on a date tomorrow. But I am playing it very cool and absolutely no one knows how excited I feel about it. My days of blabbing my every emotion to the world are over. I am not a soppy Labrador any more. I am a mysterious cat-type person. I have surprised myself with my acting skills. I may go professional. Agreed, this morning Ned saw me having a little dance and singing a love song in my mirror when he strolled past my bedroom. Naturally, because he is my younger brother, he jeered. But I had the last laugh because he didn't know *why* I was doing the little dance. Ha ha! And that means he knows nothing. So there.

'Rani,' I said as she headed for the bedroom door.

'What? Don't say anything more about you-know-who or I shall die.'

'I won't. Don't have a stressy-fit.'

'I am *not* having a stressy-fit.'

'You sure about that?' Chloe asked.

'Yes. I *am* sure about that, thank you.'

'OK, if you say so. You are *not* having a stressy-fit about possibly seeing Kenny tomorrow.'

'Correct. Now can I go please?'

'Rani.'

'What?!'

'Aren't you going to take that face mask off?'

Heh, heh. Rani could not hide her feelings like me. I am Miss Inscrutable. Even Chloe, who is painting my toenails as I write, cannot fathom my secret emotions.

7.45 p.m.

As Chloe was leaving, not long after Rani, Ned suddenly appeared in front of us on the landing. He began to gyrate in strange awkward jerks and make strangled-cat noises.

'What on earth are you doing, Ned?' Chloe asked, astonished.

'Are you practising for your part in *Joseph and the Amazing Technicolour Dreamcoat*? I added.

'Nope. I'm doing my imitation of Carrie. It's her I-love-my-*boy*friend-I-want-to-*kiss*-him-I-am-so-*luck*y-he-must-be-*bli*-ind dance.'

I need to have that conversation with Mum and Dad about the marvellous advantages of boarding school for boys. *Again.* They must understand he needs to go immediately if he wants to get the full benefit. Still, I can't wait for the date tomorrow.

RANI'S TIP • • • • • • • • • • • • • • • • • • •

If you are blessed with a large frontage, avoid big thick-knit sweaters. You may believe that they cover them up and make them less noticeable. You are wrong. Great big knits equal great big bazookas.

Chapter 2

Must do some of those exercises and have teeny tiny French bum in time for my date this afternoon.

10.30 a.m.

Bored with exercise.

I will just have to accept my bum will not be teeny tiny by two o'clock this afternoon. And I don't care. It's half-term and you can't be expected to strain yourself too much in the holidays. I deserve a well-earned rest from double English with Mrs McGuy. I will see her flash her laser-stare and crack her gnarled knuckles soon enough.

By my reckoning I have just exercised off the calorific value of an olive. We are having pizza for lunch today so I can eat it confident that I've worked most of it off already. Then Mum is dropping me at The Coffee Bean. *He* will be there. It's a pre-date date. We're meeting up with everyone else first and then going for a walk in the park on our own. It will be like a romantic film.

I can hardly believe it. After an unsettled period with frequent thunderstorms, I feel like the clouds have parted and the sun has come out on my life. (Mrs McGuy – read it and weep – I can be sooo deep.)

When I need therapy in later life (and there is no way I won't) Dr Jennings, my future therapist, will want to know there *were* good times. Imagine her joy that, *at last,* things were on the up for that fragile but brave soul, known as me, Carrie Henderson.

Here are my good things:

I have the best, best friends in the world. Lovely, lovely Chloe and Rani. And our new American friend, Maddy, who started Boughton High this term. She started off seriously scary but has decided we're OK now. Chloe and Rani were nearly *not* best friends with each other, due to recent misunderstandings about Chloe's birthday surprise. We turned a little neglected attic room in her flat into a pretty white bedroom and somehow managed to keep it a secret from her, no thanks to Rani and Chloe's boyfriend, Tom. They were so hopeless about lying, it was no surprise that Chloe imagined something was going on between them. Madness, of course. When we were in primary school and Doug Brennan used to call Chloe 'mop head' because of her curly hair and make her cry, who was it who poured the poster paint in his wellies at break? Rani. Now that's loyalty.

Not to mention that Tom worships Chloe and is the world's most devoted boyfriend.

Did I just write the word boyfriend again? Hem, hem. I think that brings me neatly on to good thing number two: I have a boyfriend of my own. A proper one. Not like Danny who kissed like a vacuum cleaner and went to live in Birmingham. And not like Chris Jones (also known as 'Chris Jones – School God') who I snogged (without passion) twice and who turned out to be such a complete jerk. My new boyfriend is kind, funny and *très*, *très* gorgeous. And he likes ME. (Quite a crucial element in a boyfriend/girlfriend scenario I have discovered.) He is called Jack Harper and even writing his name in this sentence makes me feel a bit funny. And I write his name quite a lot. It's OK between the secret covers of this diary, but I keep doodling it over exercise book covers and on scraps of paper. Then I either have to scribble over it or tear the paper up into tiny pieces and throw them in the bin. This is because I do not have a normal life, with privacy, like other girls my age. Ned stalks the landing and my mother's radar is firmly fixed on 'Carrie has a boyfriend – must have more information' at the moment. I can practically hear her blipping when she walks past my door.

And finally: *LES FRANÇAISES ARRIVERENT*. Which I think means 'The French girls are coming.' Our French exchange programme starts soon. Some of us are disappointed that the boys' exchanges aren't coming too. Due to an 'incident' last year, culminating in Sophie Willis's dad marching up to the school with two of his mates from the darts team, looking for 'some French poof called Pierre', this year Boughton High is playing it safe. Just our luck. However, Madame Debas, head of French, has a friend who teaches at some smart private girls' school in Paris and she's arranged for fourteen girls to come over to us this year.

So I'm sure they are going to be, what did Rani say? – '*Chic* and *belle*.'

Though Middleton is our nearest town, and this part of England is not known as a centre of either *chic*-ness or *belle*-ness, we do our best, Chloe especially, who dresses with wit and charm on next to nothing. She customises fantastic bargains from second-hand shops. She could walk down the street anywhere in the world and get admiring glances. And no one can make more magical things happen with hair and make-up than Rani. Me, I try my best and like to think I'm not bad at interior design. But we are only three fourteen-year-old girls against the masses. So the thought of real cosmopolitan style arriving on our doorstep is very exciting. We'll be able to share fashion and make-up tips and everything.

Vive la France!

12.30 p.m.

Mum has just appeared to say we're going now. Yes, we are actually going OUT to have a pizza, in Middleton, to a place with waitresses and chocolate fudge cake for pudding and mints in a bowl. I know normal families eat out all the time but it wouldn't even qualify for an annual event in our household. Imaginary therapist Dr Jennings, please take note: deprived childhood.

12.35 p.m.

Ned has walked past my bedroom door with his nearly thirteen-year-old bum hanging out of his jeans. Revolting. I don't *want* to see his boxers all the time, thank you very much. And I certainly don't want to see them doing that stupid dance every time he goes past. Mum says to ignore him, it's just an annoying phase he's going through. Well, it seems to have lasted since birth.

Now my big brother Max has gone travelling for a year I have to shoulder the burden of trying to crush Ned's spirit all on my own. It's gruelling work, but someone has to do it.

12.40 p.m.

Had to come back up. Forgot my mobile and had to check what I looked like one more time as well. Six foot tall (at my age!), long dark blonde hair, blue eyes, black denim mini and slouchy boots.

Not bad at all if I say so myself, because shapeless, bendy tube legs are encased in forgiving black tights.

Now I've been downstairs, I would like to add to my trials: Mum's maroon acrylic cardigan and comfy stretch trousers. Having a parent who is a stranger to natural fibres – that's quite a cross to bear for a young girl. Add the fact she's deputy head of my school and I think anyone could see why I'll be spending a lot of time lying on that therapy couch.

CARRIE'S TIP • • • • • • • • • • • • • • • • • • •

If you do have a really big bum, never wear jackets that stop on it. Also never wear high-waisted trousers — they make your bum look huuuge (Mum, take note). I'm not even going to say anything about elasticated waists because no one under sixty-five has any reason to be going there.

You need a full-length mirror to see what you look like from top to toe. It only needs a narrow space and brings light into your bedroom. Mirrors make small rooms look bigger.

Chapter 3

Jack was waiting for me outside the café, looking gorgeous in a black jacket and jeans. His brown eyes went smiley when he saw me, and that made my stomach flip over. Like it always does.

Chloe, Tom and Maddy were already in The Coffee Bean. I noticed Chloe was wearing the stunning suede designer boots that Maddy had given her for her birthday. Chloe had lent her old pair to Jennifer Cooper when we did a makeover on her. Jennifer had been trying to impress Jack. Maddy had been trying to impress Sasha Dooley and her friends by pretending she could drink a lot of Bacardi. Result: she was sick on Chloe's old boots. Jennifer never really got over it, but Maddy learned a lesson. She vows she'll never drink alcohol again.

Maddy was in a long black felt coat that you just knew was by a big Japanese designer. Her dad is Daniel Van de Velde, the fashion writer and guru, and he gets sent loads of freebies from designers. Lucky her. She's got wardrobes of clothes but has only just started to wear them. When she first came to the area, she was in a strange place style-wise. Let's just say her look involved a lot of black and white make-up and ripped tights. She looked very unfit and bulgy then. Rani rashly suggested we jog with her in the mornings before school to help her get fit and she *is* looking so much better – more statuesque and imposing rather than wild and scary. Thankfully she has the confidence to run on her own now. She was miles faster than Rani or me and it was pretty obvious from the first day that we were holding her back. The shame. (Memo to self: must find method of getting fit, which does not involve getting up early or, preferably, exercise.)

Jack and I got our hot chocolates and shuffled up next to Maddy.

'Rani still at Kenny's?' I asked, looking around the crowded café.

'Yes,' Tom replied. 'Florence Nightingale has at last been allowed access.'

'In other words, Kenny's getting over his bug and his mum says that he's well enough to have visitors,' Chloe elaborated.

Jack began twisting a strand of my hair around his fingers. I swear everyone could hear my heart beating.

'Has he been able to do any revision?' Chloe asked anxiously.

Revision. I hate that word. This is the first time we've seen the boys this half-term. They've been sweating away at GCSEs for what seems like for ever now. And the worse part is that Jack's dad is going on a business trip and so it's been arranged that Jack's going to stay with his mother in the depths of the countryside. She normally swans about between London and Paris but has been persuaded to do her motherly duty and help out. So he'll be revising hard for a week with Tom who's going with him.

'You're all heart, aren't you, Tom?' I said, thinking to myself that if Jack got the bug he might not go away. What were the chances of getting Jack to kiss Kenny in the next few days? Slim. But then I checked myself. I knew they had to work. I mustn't be selfish. 'You'll miss the arrival of the French girls, of course.'

'Know any more about the Paris posse yet?' Jack asked.

'I know mine is called Marie-Camille, but that's about it.

They've posted us letters that should arrive soon. We wrote to them and they have to reply.'

'What did you say in your letter?' Maddy asked. She wasn't going to have a French girl – she does Spanish – but was interested in what they'd be like.

'You know, the usual. What I like to do, about my family, blah, blah, blah. I felt it sounded pretty boring really. It's very difficult to convey your fascinating life and personality in a foreign language.'

'I totally agree,' a voice above me said. 'It's so hard to say:

a) my dad's a paranoid control-freak who hates boys;

b) my mum's obsessed with the local amateur dramatic society's forthcoming production of *My Fair Lady*; and

c) my brother has a pathological terror of girls;

with a French vocabulary of about nine words. Move over, Tom.'

Rani had arrived. After she had assured us that Kenny was definitely on the mend but no, not snoggable yet, thank you for asking, she continued, 'I'm worried they're going to think we're boring. I mean they live in *Paris*, for God's sake. It's caviar and champagne up the Eiffel Tower every night for them. What does Boughton High have to offer?'

'We *are* taking them to London for the day,' Chloe soothed.

I leaned forward. 'Actually, I have just been given a huuuuuge hint over my pizza by Mum that the school has thought of something exciting for us to do when they're here.' I sat back smugly.

'Whey-hey! Like what?' Chloe asked excitedly.

My smug look slipped a bit. 'Well she wouldn't say exactly *what*. Mum just looked sort of secretive and said she thought the school had planned an interesting project to keep us all busy.'

Rani looked slightly deflated. 'I wonder what that will be.'

I had no idea, and to be truthful Mum and I aren't necessarily on the same wavelength as to what thrills the soul, but I thought I should mention it anyway. Mum did look very pleased with herself when she said it, and miracles do happen.

'She told me we'll find out as soon as we get back to school.'

Tom started gnashing his teeth. 'It's so unfair. A crowd of fit French girls are arriving and we'll miss most of their visit. Never mind, we shall still have – what do the French call you? Oh yes, *les rosbifs*. Yes, our roast beef girls.' And he put his arm affectionately around Chloe's shoulders, who could not look less like a *rosbif*, and he knew it. She rolled her eyes at me.

'Hey, if Chloe's a *rosbif*, you know what that makes you?' I said, quick as a flash.

'What?'

'A Yorkshire pudding!' I am floored by my own wit sometimes.

'Why do men go so crazy about French girls, I'd like to know?' Chloe sighed, unfloored. It can be hard when your friend's sense of humour is not as finely tuned as your own. 'What is so special about them?'

'Well, Jack's the man to ask,' I said helpfully. 'He's been to Paris recently.'

Jack's mum had left his dad for some fancy lord and the two of them were now living between Paris and London.

He put his hands behind his head, leaned back and grinned mischievously. 'Ah yes, those French girls ... Well, it can't be denied; they do have a certain *je ne sais quoi*.'

I hit him with my teaspoon. 'Name three things that are so great about French girls.'

'Only three?' he gasped incredulously. I hit him again.

'Allow me to start,' Tom interrupted. 'Great flirts, very sexy.'

'How do you know?' Chloe wailed. 'You've never been to France. I mean, have you ever even *met* a Frenchwoman?'

Tom hunched his shoulders, hurt. 'I will have you know that I am in possession of a telly and I have seen French *films.*'

'Well, that's not the same,' I groaned. 'That's like saying you know what all English girls are like because you've seen Keira Knightly, or what all American girls are like because you've seen Paris Hilton on TV.'

Tom looked serious and gazed into my eyes. 'All American girls *do* look like Paris Hilton, Carrie. And never tell me otherwise. OK?'

Maddy gave him one of her more scary looks. And that's pretty scary. Chloe also gave him a hard stare and said, 'I'm going to pretend I never heard that because otherwise I will have to admit to myself that my boyfriend is beyond stupid.'

Tom beamed.

'They *do* tend to dress well,' Maddy said. 'When I lived in Paris, you really did notice it. No one looks scruffy, no one has messy hair. I'm trying to remember if I saw anyone with spots . . .'

We were all looking at her after that.

'You lived in Paris!' Chloe looked enviously at her.

'Yes, when I was younger. My dad was working there. He needed to spend some time working with the European fashion houses and he edited a fashion magazine.'

'You never said!' I gasped. She is constantly surprising, that girl.

'I don't know why, it just never came up before. And it was a while ago. Then we went back to Los Angeles before coming here. He does say the Paris girls always look smart.'

As I had just dripped a blob of hot chocolate on my new

black denim miniskirt I found this talk of looking smart a bit depressing. Perhaps it is just as well Jack isn't going to be here the whole time. All that shiny hair and *chic* outfits plus the sexy flirting . . . and we haven't even mentioned the accents. And Jack, with his intense, poetic good looks is such a fabulous specimen of English manhood. I am beginning to feel glad that he will be living on the side of a craggy, wet Welsh mountain, though I am going to miss him horribly. It sounds as if we are going to have our hands full with these girls. We won't have time for a love life.

Now I must write about the next (and best) bit of the day. Drat. Have to do it later – Mum is calling Ned and me downstairs. I will wait till Ned goes down first. If I hear that voice caterwauling 'Baby, I love you' one more time I will not be responsible for my actions.

 CHLOE'S TIP · · · · · · · · · · · · · · · · · · ·

To make sure your legs always look as long as possible (Carrie is lucky she doesn't have to worry about this) always make sure your trouser hem touches the ground when wearing trousers with a heel. Trouser ends flapping several inches above the ground instantly make your legs look stumpy.

Chapter 4

So – I *slightly* assaulted Ned.

I didn't plan to, but I was quietly eating a banana and he got this distant look on his face next to me and started crooning softly, but just so I could hear.

'I may be a beanpole,

As desperate as could be,

But at last I've found a moron,

Who will go out with me . . .*Watch me dance!*'

He yelled the last bit as loudly as he could, threw his arms up into the air and starting waving them wildly, like he was at a rave.

Have been in my room for some time now. Mum said to reflect on the fact that violence is never the answer and what will Marie-Camille think of that sort of behaviour? I tried to argue that a bit of banana on your nose is hardly violence, but Mum wasn't going to listen. It wasn't my fault; I was provoked beyond reason. I think Dr Jennings will be shocked that my parents don't take this sort of suffering more seriously. Brothers and sisters can be like Chinese water torture – it's the constant, tiny drip, drip, drip of irritation. It's obvious you're going to go mad in the end. Dad has threatened Ned with skateboard confiscation if he carries on with the dance/singing thing so I know he'll stop. But of course, the damage to my spirit is already done.

This is why I can't wait to have another girl actually living in the same house. She'll be my ally against Ned. Like a twin sister. I'm going to get out my magazine stash and put ones I think she'd like aside. I wonder if she'd be cool about swapping clothes? Best not rush her on that one.

9.45 p.m.

Right. Back to the most important thing today: my date.

After I'd got the hot chocolate off my skirt, Jack and I left The Coffee Bean and went for a walk – just us. He held my hand and it was soooo romantic. And he is taller than me, which is rare in a boy, so just the right size for walking next to. When I'm with him I never have to think too hard about what to say, or worry if there's a silence, because he makes everything funny and interesting. And, unlike Chris Jones, he asks *you* questions about what *you* feel about things. So we were strolling along under the trees, the June sunlight piercing through the dancing leaves and their shadows playing on the path ahead of us, and I was telling him how excited I was about Marie-Camille coming and Jack was saying. 'So, have I got this right? Next week you're going to get a letter from *your* one —'

'*Your* one? What's this? Ooooh – then which is *my* one?' We both spun round and right behind us was a smirking Jennifer Cooper. She continued to answer her own question. 'The totally gorgeous one, I think.' She was hanging on to Chris Jones's arm like it was a lifebelt off the *Titanic*. I don't think she had let go since they got together at the school fund-raising dance. The only reason she will accept for him not seeing her is revising. Not known for his studious nature in the past, now he seems to be always at his books. Well, tucked safely away at home, anyway.

He gave me a sheepish smile. Jennifer frowned. Her pale blonde hair was swept over her eyes in the style Rani had given her. She was wearing a short skirt and boots she'd never have been seen in before we did her makeover.

I explained. 'We're talking about the French exchanges, Jennifer.' (Not that it's any of your business, I wanted to add – but didn't.)

Jennifer immediately looked bored. 'Don't remind me. Mine's called Katia. Sooo tedious. I can't bear to think about having her around. And I'm going to be so sad now Chris is locking himself away with his books for ever and ever.' She cooed up at him. 'What a drag, having a distraction from thinking about you every minute.' She gave him this gooey look.

Jack didn't catch my eye because he knew I might get the giggles. Thankfully Jennifer had clearly decided our little chat was over. Chris managed a weak grin and a pointy click with the finger and, 'See yah,' before she propelled him firmly towards the bandstand.

'And to think she could have been mine.' Jack sighed deeply and put his arm around my shoulder.

I deserved this. It was a reminder of a painful period in my life when I thought I liked Chris and I had tried to match-make Jack and Jennifer. Luckily Jack wasn't interested in her, and Chris Jones soon proved what a jerk *he* was.

'Yup. Could have been me that she doesn't let out of her sight. She may be a very pretty girl since you three worked your magic, but if that relationship lasts till the end of term I'll be amazed. She finds out where our lessons are and peers through the glass, glaring at all the Year Eleven girls. They're sick of it. A man can only take so much, but I actually think he's a bit frightened of her.'

'He's so vain I can't imagine him being afraid of anyone.'

'I don't know,' Jack grinned. 'I think he was seriously scared the day you slugged him across the back of his head with your school bag.'

'I think I would prefer to forget that incident,' I said stiffly.

I had just found out he had snogged another classmate, Jet, behind my back. What girl wouldn't have been annoyed? However it was Jennifer, not Jet, who scooped him up at the dance.

'Jennifer is more than welcome to him. Ever since we did that makeover on her she's been impossible. She speaks to me in this condescending tone now as if she's completely forgotten we gave her a hand. I don't want grovelling gratitude but I can do without the smugness.'

'I think it's more that she suspects you secretly burn with jealousy over her going out with Chris.'

'I *know* and it's so irritating. Can't she see that I'm —?' Whoops. I nearly lost my head and said, 'Can't she see that I'm completely and totally crazy about you?' Luckily I stopped just in time. How uncool would that be?

'Can't she see you're what?' He was smiling at me.

I took a deep breath and exhaled. 'Can't-she-see-that-I'm-going-out-with-*someone-else*?'

Jack raised his eyebrows a fraction and nodded sagely.

'I think she imagines you're going out with me just to make Chris jealous.'

'As if!'

'So why are you going out with me then?' He was looking straight at me with those deep dark eyes and he got my arms and wrapped them around his waist.

And I wanted to say the truth about all the things I felt about him but instead I shrugged my shoulders in a fake-casual way and said, 'Why do *you* go out with *me*?'

How totally pathetic was that? I had an inward cringe.

He sighed deeply and frowned.

'Now why would I be going out with you? Why indeed?' His eyes widened. 'I wonder why myself.' He looked serious. 'No, I'm kidding. You know why, don't you?'

I shook my head.

'Shall I tell you?' He brushed my hair back off my face.

I nodded.

He raised his eyes to the sky. 'It's because, it's because . . .'

My heart was pounding . . . I was staring intently at his face. This was it. He looked straight back at me, looking like he was struggling to find the words . . .

I could hardly breathe.

'Nah,' he sighed and slowly shook his head with a wicked grin. 'It's gone.'

Chris and Jennifer had looked startled to see me chasing him down the path trying to hit him repeatedly with a twig before we both fell over in hysterics into the rhododendrons.

I think I might be falling in love. Seriously.

**MADDY'S TIP** • • • • • • • • • • • • • • • •

If you are tall like Carrie, don't be tempted to slouch, thinking that it makes you look smaller. It doesn't. Imagine there's a string coming out of your head, pulling you up. This trick makes anyone, whatever their height, instantly look better.

Chapter 5

At last I have escaped to my room for ten minutes. Mum has gone completely mental.

She went into Max's room this morning and came out with a fixed expression on her face.

She has deemed it unfit for habitation by visiting French people.

When you are a girl who really likes a boy, you don't want to be bothered about clearing out rooms. You want to hang out in your bedroom and sing to yourself and write in your diary. And check your phone for text messages that you may have missed even though the phone is never more than two inches away from your person. At all times.

Even in the loo. Though that can be a bit awkward.

'Carrie!' Mum snapped at me earlier. 'I can see you watching my lips moving but you're not listening to a word I say. Will you please come back to earth? We – are – going – to – clear – out – Max's – room.'

Dad and Ned have been roped in too. They were not pleased. I am concerned this may engender a less than positive attitude towards my soon-to-be new best friend.

Ned removed his broken skateboards, old trainers, magazines and computer games. Mum picked up the growing pile of her clothes from the cross-trainer that served as her extra wardrobe. Dad removed his abdominals-toner (also never used – as the strains on his shirt buttons testify).

I took out all the My Little Pony albums and toys that I had stored there because they might be worth something one day. I have great plans to wow them on the *Antiques Roadshow* in a few years. Mum I bought a new blue check duvet cover and curtains and a white rug for the floor. I painted the old pine wardrobe white and decorated it by painting two delicate bunches of forget-me-nots on each door panel. Then Mum let me paint Max's old wicker chair white too and I am going to use an old, worn pair of jeans to make some small cushions for it. It is going to look really pretty. I'm sure Marie-Camille will appreciate all our efforts when she arrives. I wonder what Dr Jennings's opinions are on child labour. Not *très* pro, I should imagine.

And no time at all till Jack goes away. We could be in the park now holding hands and having a competition about how many songs we can think of with the word 'baby' in it (or 'blue' or 'girl' – don't bother with 'love', it's too easy and a tiny bit embarrassing at our stage of the relationship). Actually, we couldn't be in the park. He's gone to London to see the play they're doing for English. His mum is there for a few days before she goes to the country house. I won't get to see him again until I wave off his train to Wales on Saturday. We are star-crossed lovers. Or Mum-crossed, or something.

Mum has found me. Off to the workhouse.

12.00 a.m.
We cleaned: of which I have had a lot of experience since we did the makeover on Chloe's room and believe me, the novelty does wear off.

12.15 p.m.

Rani just rang to say that the parents of her exchange had just rung to check that Cécile (for such is the name of her French girl) would have a room to play her musical instruments in, as they didn't want her falling behind with her music practice. Rani says her own parents are already impressed.

'They say I might learn so much from her,' Rani moaned.

'Well, she sounds great. I know I'm really looking forward to having mine to stay.'

'So you keep saying. And I keep saying I hope she's not going to be a disappointment.'

'Not a chance. She's going to be my French kindred spirit. Now tell me, when are you going to see Kenny again?'

'Think I might go round tomorrow.'

'You might sound more excited about it.'

'I am excited about it. I do really like him.' Rani's voice trailed off.

'What's up?'

'Nothing.'

'I'll say it again, my feisty pal, "What's up?" I know your slightly anxious voice by now. The really nice boy who has been mad about you for ages is soon to be out and about and kissable, and there's something bothering you. What is it?'

'Nothing.'

'We could waste a lot of time going round the houses like this. Come on, Rani, spit it out.'

'OK, if you must know I'm just a little nervous about the er . . . er . . .'

'The lippy-clinch bit?'

'Yup, that bit.'

So I gave her the talk that Chloe had once given me about when it's the right person it tends to be all right and clashing noses, etc. just don't matter, but I could tell she was still agitated.

'You know, Rani, if you don't feel ready to kiss him, don't.'

'Really?' I could hear the relief in her voice.

'Look, I know Chloe and I have been going on and on about it and teasing you. And maybe we've not been too sensitive about your feelings on this. We just assumed you wanted to.'

'I know, but it's my fault as well. I kind of went along with it and thought that I really wanted to because I thought I should, and you and Chloe both have boyfriends now . . . I do like him a lot but, well, he's always fun and relaxed when people are around but when it's just us he goes so shy and that makes me shy somehow and it's just uuurgh . . . so embarrassing.'

'Rani,' I said firmly. 'Rani, you mustn't do anything you don't feel like. Especially not because of Chloe and me. Kenny really likes you; he likes hanging around with you. He thinks you're funny and clever, which you are. It doesn't have to be anything more than friends if you don't want it to be.'

'But what if that means I'm going to die a lonely old woman in a crumbling tower block with just my twelve cats for company?'

'Yeah, right, like that's going to happen.'

'I just don't want to get left behind.'

'Left behind! Bloody hell, Rani, we've hardly started! How can you talk about being left behind? And anyway, since when have you ever been swayed by anyone else? You're the most independent thinker I know. Don't let us down by getting all bothered by what other people are doing at this stage in the game. Chloe and

I will feel we have been conned and have to sue you for being our friend under false pretences or something.'

'You're right. I'm making a big deal out of nothing. I'm in charge of what I do or do not decide to do.'

'Exactly. And anyway if he kisses anything like Danny you'd be well out of it.'

'And what about Jack?'

But I changed the subject because I just didn't feel it was the right moment to tell her what kissing Jack was like.

And so we talked about the London trip instead and what we wanted to do there.

Rani said she's going to make a London To Do list and stop worrying about kissing anybody.

I feel I have done a good day's work.

Dr Jennings would be proud of me.

If I wasn't going to be an interior designer I *could* be a therapist.

 RANI'S TIP ●

For kissable lips (only if that's what you want) keep lip-gloss to the middle of the lips only. If you apply it thickly all over it can give you the dreaded clown look - as can putting lip-liner outside the corners of your mouth.

Chapter 6

Chère *Carrie,*

*My name is Marie-Camille De Villiers. I live in a large apart-
ment in Paris near the Galeries Lafayette. My father is the
director of a large Swiss bank and you perhaps know my
mother – she is the actress Jacqueline Breton. She has been in
many films. She travels the world. She has many parties and
knows many people. I like to go shopping in the Champs Élysées
and I like to go riding in the Bois de Boulogne. We take holidays
in St Tropez, the Maldives and the Seychelles. My favourite shops
are D&G, Kenzo and Cyrillus for everyday shopping. My mother
takes me to Dior and Valentino where she has her clothes made
for her. I love fashion. I went to London with my mother last year
to buy clothes. We are very close. I have not sister or brothers.*

Will your older brother be home when I visit?

Marie-Camille

I read it out to Chloe and Rani. We had piled up the little staircase
that leads into Chloe's lovely bedroom (for which I do take some
responsibility – hem, hem). We had made a den on Chloe's bed
and pulled the white sari canopies around us. Then we'd opened
our letters and a packet of biscuits.

I had showed the letter to Mum when it arrived this morning.
She'd raised her eyebrows at the last bit.

'She does sound, er . . . grown up, doesn't she?' She had looked thoughtful. 'I have heard of Jacqueline Breton – she was very famous about fifteen years ago. I'm not sure if she's done anything lately. She certainly was very beautiful. Sounds like they live a very luxurious life.'

'What did you put for what you liked to do?' Chloe asked.

The shame.

'Reading, interior design and seeing my friends. How lame does that sound?'

'Not lame at all,' Chloe said sharply. 'Better than having your interests as shopping and getting off with people's brothers.'

'Ooooooh, OK,' I trilled. 'Keep your hair on.'

Chloe grinned. 'Sorry, didn't mean to snap, it's just interesting what comes over as important to her.'

'She does sound a bit snooty,' Rani added.

'Rubbish,' I said briskly. 'I don't think that at all. I think she's just keen to share her world with me. I'm sure she's going to be great. She certainly sounds very stylish. It'll be cool. I'm going to learn so much from her.'

Rani gave a snort. I ignored it.

Of course it was going to be all right. It was going to be fantastic having such a knowledgeable, sophisticated exchange person. Maybe they were a bit jealous.

Rani read out her letter from Cécile.

Chère *Rani*,

What a pretty name! I am very much looking forward to meeting you and all your friends. I know we shall have fun together. I live with my parents and older sister. She has just won a

music scholarship to the most academic college in Paris. My
parents are both international lawyers. After school I do music
and drama. I play the violin, the piano and the clarinet. When
we come to England we have to do a project about our visit.
This will be fun.
Cécile

'P.S.' I continued. 'We are all geniuses and incredibly beautiful . . .'

'Carrie!' Chloe chided. 'You're the one going on about being positive.'

'I know. I'm sorry, I just feel I'm wasting my life not having two Oxford degrees and grade eight tambourine under my belt already.'

'I know what you mean,' Rani said thoughtfully. 'I do self-defence but it sounds a bit feeble in comparison. Do you think she's going to feel there's not enough to do here?'

'Are you kidding? She'll be glad of the rest, by the sounds of it. Are all these French girls rich and talented?' I asked.

'Well, mine is called Agathe and she sounds completely normal.' Chloe scanned through her letter. 'Nope, no instruments or mention of any after-school activities; lives with her two younger brothers and her mum. Mum works in "cloth" – don't know what that means. Fabric shop? Maybe she knows loads about fashion. No mention of her dad living with them. Maybe they're divorced – like mine.'

'She does sound normal,' I agreed with a touch of envy. Then I pulled myself together. Marie-Camille was going to be great. How could she not love my friends for a start?

Admittedly my family were a drawback. Ned and Dad were

continuing with their negative vibe, and Mum's fashion sense always takes a bit of getting used to by newcomers, but I feel confident we'll all be all right in the end.

'So it looks like Carrie's got the Paris Princess, Chloe's got the Best-dressed and I've got Miss Perfect,' Rani sighed.

'Still feeling positive psychic feelings now, Carrie?' Chloe grinned.

'Yes,' I said firmly.

And on that note I am going downstairs to make myself some tea.

8.00 p.m.

Jack comes back from London late tonight. I'm going to see him off tomorrow. Hoping for a romantic farewell scene. I wonder if he'll say anything to reveal his feelings as we whisper our goodbyes?

Saturday 2.15 p.m.

Jack has gone and I am already missing him way too much. Mum gave Chloe and me a lift to the station. She wouldn't wait in the car like I pleaded, and then when we saw Tom and Jack they were in the middle of about one hundred students from a language school saying goodbyes too. Polish people are very emotional sometimes. Then they all got on to the train as well, so it wasn't quite the dramatic farewell I had envisaged with him hanging out of the window clasping my outstretched hand, fingertips touching as the whistle blew, etc, etc. Tom and Chloe have been going out so long that they were quite relaxed about it all. Jack and I didn't get a moment in private. Jack's dad, Mr Harper, is a nice enough man but I wouldn't want to declare my feelings in front of him. Let alone snog anyone. And he and Mum did hang around so. Luckily our relationship is strong enough to survive these setbacks.

I would like to discuss with Dr Jennings the fact that missing someone is another VERY BAD FEELING. One that is only natural to want to avoid. I suspect she may say that he is only going for a week, and think about people who have to say goodbye to loved ones (OK, not allowed to say the L-word yet – *really*, really *liked* ones) for ages and ages. I'm not going to go all stupid and droop away in my room. I am not a child any more, but I will be glad when Marie-Camille comes and we're busy and my mind will be occupied. At the moment, all it is occupied with is wanting to see Jack and the sound of Ned muttering under his breath as he passes the bathroom and sees the space he's been forced to make on the shelves for Marie-Camille. The bulk of his skateboard magazine collection has been re-housed in the garage. He is not pleased. He is down to vital issues only and there have been tough choices to be made. Am now seriously concerned about his negative attitude towards her. I do not want this to spoil her stay.

4.00 p.m.
Wrote to Jack. Kept it bright and breezy. Lots about how I'm looking forward to Marie-Camille coming (so he understands I am an independent girl and my life goes on without him). Feel sad though. Mustn't feel sad. It's only for a couple of weeks. What would Dr J say? Think positive.

Rani and Chloe and I have phoned each other to distract

ourselves from boys-gone-away depression. And I want to know what they're wearing tomorrow.

After getting advice from Chloe at her place the other day, I am going for skinny grey cords tucked into black boots, tight, white long-sleeved T-shirt and small grey cardigan, lots of black beads around my neck and my long hair up. Rani, true to her word still says she is coming in baggy black sweater and black mini. She is going to wear her huge black sunglasses even though I pointed out that the weather forecast for tomorrow isn't great and she won't need them. Chloe decided on a tiny flower-print floaty dress over a very thin pale green wool top and jeans with several ribbons tied around her waist. We will not let the good name of the Style Sisters down! (Though Rani's sunglasses are borderline.)

 CARRIE'S TIP • • • • • • • • • • • • • • • • • •

Always take your friends with you when you are trying on glasses and sunglasses. They can see what suits your face better than you.

If they don't come with a case to put them in (or you've lost it), smaller pencil cases work well and stop lenses getting scratched in your bag.

Chapter 7

Well, she's here. My French kindred spirit. She is in Max's room and I am having a much needed lie down.

We all met in the school car park to await the arrival of the coach. Rani kept bumping into people until Chloe persuaded her that pushing your sunglasses on to the top of your head was really cool. I could see Melanie and Jet trying to sneer at Chloe's outfit and only managing to look green with envy. Poor Jet in her top-to-toe designer wear. She couldn't pull off an original look if she tried. Instead, belted and expensively buckled in an orange suit she looked over-dressed in an outfit much too old for her. I will say this though: at least it matched her tan. Harsh words, but the truth must be told.

Her mum was there in yellow miniskirt and matching stilettos standing next to mine who was in a navy pleated nylon skirt and pink sweatshirt with purple butterflies on. Flying the flag for British style.

AT LAST! The coach arrived and we were jumping up and down trying to look in through the windows. Madame Debas, also known as The Rottweiler, also known as head of French, was there to tick them off her list as they appeared and point them in the direction of the right girl from Boughton High.

The first girl off the coach was a tall, elegant blonde with an air of total confidence wearing a cashmere sweater, pale cords and smart leather loafers. She patted a silk scarf twisted elegantly around her neck.

'Suffering sophistication!' Rani gasped. 'Do you think that they're all like that? Oh hell's bells, she's looking at me!'

And indeed she was. She gave Rani a charming smile and came over and kissed her lightly on both cheeks. And then did an extra one. While Rani was recovering, Cécile politely introduced herself to Rani's mum. Mrs Ray was dead impressed. We had barely time to get to grips with the kissing thing, when Chloe noticed a mousy girl hovering at her side. She was small, as small as Rani and dressed in a green sweatshirt and shapeless brown trousers that stopped ten centimetres above her ankles, revealing short white socks and sturdy black lace up shoes. Her long light brown hair was pulled back into a rubber band and her grey eyes peered anxiously at Chloe. I could see Rani was mentally putting blusher and mascara on her.

'Hi,' Chloe gathered herself together and beamed warmly. 'Are you Agathe?'

The girl bit her bottom lip and nodded.

'Brilliant! I'm Chloe, great to meet you.' Chloe gave her a quick hug but the girl looked rather relieved when Chloe released her and introduced her to her mother and younger brother, Jim. Jim proceeded to give her a huge hug and a big kiss on the cheek. Jim has Down's Syndrome and Chloe watched nervously because, although she had mentioned it in her letter, sometimes people can be quite stupid about meeting anyone who they think aren't exactly the same as them (and who is exactly the same as anyone else anyway?). Agathe looked down at the tarmac, her face scarlet. Chloe's expression clouded momentarily until

Agathe raised her eyes and Chloe saw it was an embarrassed and pleased scarlet. Agathe then looked up and gave Jim a big grin. Style or no style, Agathe and Chloe were going to get on.

Obviously during all of this I was hopping from one foot to the other waiting to catch sight of Marie-Camille but it seemed everyone else was pairing up but me.

I was distracted by Jennifer, who had been staring at Agathe.

'My God,' she said loudly, 'I thought the French were supposed to know something about style. If mine looks like that I'm refusing to have her.'

Chloe, who had turned to take Agathe to collect her bags, turned and pulled an outraged face at me.

Seconds later, a large smiling girl in baggy denim dungarees, T-shirt and a mass of red curls came pounding up and queried 'Jennifer?' loudly in her face.

Jennifer blanched and opened her mouth to say something but all that came out were two pathetic little coughs. Katia gave her a big slap on the back.

I was enjoying this merry scene when Rani nudged me and pointed to the door of the coach.

And there was Marie-Camille. It could only have been her. Peering over a pair of whimper-inducingly cool sunglasses, she surveyed the chaos around her. Everything about her screamed expensive. But not in a Jet way. This girl was sophistication on a stick. You just knew she'd never been to TopShop or Hennes in her life. She was elegant, slim and graceful. Her dark brown hair was cut into the shiniest bob I had ever seen outside of a magazine, her heart-shaped face framed large brown eyes and a carefully made up rosebud mouth which pushed out in a discontented pout. In fact,

I would describe her expression as verging on pained. She carefully put her sunglasses in her shiny leather bag and leaned towards Madame who waved in my direction. She gave me a long look and I felt instantly inferior. I never thought much about where I get my hair done (Rani's) or buy my clothes (the High Street) but I thought about it then, because I could tell she had, just in that glance.

I had to admit that I felt intimidated. Which is *not* a feeling that I am that familiar with. It isn't very nice. Mum swung into action, prodding me in the back and pushing me forward. I could see Marie-Camille taking in Mum's clothes and frizzy hair and it just added to my feeling that this trip was not coming up to her expectations.

Thankfully, Marie-Camille didn't do kisses that actually made contact with your face. I don't blame her because her make-up was so perfect you wouldn't want anything to spoil it. She just pursed her lips in the general area of your cheek.

Mum held out her hand and Marie-Camille waggled the tips of Mum's fingers. This wasn't going quite as I had planned – I almost felt like dropping a curtsy. But as anyone who knows me would testify, I am not a girl for giving up when it comes to forging new relationships with people. Oh no.

'Hi,' I said and tried to look cheerful and welcoming.

'*Bonjour*,' she sighed, underwhelmed. (I think it must have been a tiring journey.) 'We discover my bags, *non*?'

And we did. She gestured towards a towering pile of Louis Vuitton luggage.

Mum asked heartily, 'Which one is yours?'

Her big brown eyes opened wide.

'*Mais, tout.*'

'All!' Mum paled. 'What? *All* of them?'

I looked at Mum anxiously. I didn't want her to make a fuss about things when the poor girl had only just arrived. It's not her fault she's rich and has tons of clothes. I'm sure in the circles she moves in, five suitcases for two weeks is no big deal.

Marie-Camille got out a powder compact from her Hermès bag. She began to re-apply her lipstick (Chanel, I noticed).

She saw us standing motionless staring at her, put her lipstick in her bag, sighed, and dangled both hands in front of her. She gave them a little shake. 'You see, I 'ave not veree strong arms for the 'eavy *bagages.*'

Mum looked sceptical.

Marie-Camille made a 'tsk tsk' sound and elaborated for our benefit. 'It is not possible for me to carry big zings. I 'ave ze arms zat are . . . 'ow do you say . . . *faible,* yes, feeble.' And she looked Mum and me up and down meaningfully. She gave her wrists another dangle.

Mum opened her mouth to say something.

'Come on, then,' I said brightly. 'Best be getting on with it.'

To my relief Mum responded to my pleading look and we headed for the buckled leather mountain. Crisis averted. Though I think I have done my back in.

Marie-Camille walked with us to the car, swinging a dainty pink leather vanity case. She raised her eyebrows at the sight of Mum gathering piles of papers and files from the back seat to clear more space. I'd never given Mum's car much thought but I admit I felt embarrassed. Although a Renault Clio and therefore French, it was obviously not what Marie-Camille was used to. After she gingerly got in she told us her dad drives a Jaguar and her mum has some thumping four-wheel drive I'd never heard of. Apparently when Marie-Camille passes her test she will get a customised powder-pink Mini Cooper convertible. I was jealous about the Mini. I could see myself in one of those. Wearing her sunglasses. Rani's mum drove past us on the way home; Rani was pressed against the window making frantic 'phone me' motions with her hand.

I'm desperate to talk to her but I've got to go and help Marie-Camille unpack and have supper first. I'm dying to see what she's got in all those cases.

7.15 p.m.

I am concerned about Mum's attitude. She does not seem to appreciate that Marie-Camille is a girl used to a very different life to ours. The High Life, I think it is called.

Mum does not understand this. Mum has developed a *tone*.

When we got back, Mum came upstairs with me to show her to her room. Dad and Ned could move the suitcases up there when they got in from PC World (their chosen place of worship on a Sunday). I couldn't wait for her to see it. We had worked so hard to get it ready. I proudly opened the door and said 'I hope you like it.'

She looked around slowly. 'Mmmm.' She gave a little nod. 'Of course, it will be fine. You must excuse me; zis is veree strange for me. In Paris I live in a big apartment. Veree big. Here, it eez veree *petit*.'

She gave us a brave smile. I didn't dare look at Mum's expression, but I guessed it wasn't joyful.

Mum said firmly, 'We all worked very hard to get this room

ready for you, Marie-Camille. We do hope you will be happy here.'

'I'm sure she will, Mum,' I said in warning. Honestly, I thought, the girl is used to a bedroom as big as our whole house, give her a break. But I admit I did feel disappointed. I thought Mum and I had done a good job making the room look pretty and fresh. Still, silly of me to think that my interior design ideas would be up to Paris jet-set standards.

Mum went back downstairs. I don't think she could trust herself not to say something.

Marie-Camille looked around the room again. 'Where eez the room for my clothes-ses?'

I walked over to the wardrobe and opened it with a flourish. 'Here.'

She went over and stuck her head right in it as if she was hoping it might suddenly expand like in *The Lion, The Witch and The Wardrobe*. I wanted to say if she kept going she might meet a faun back there, under a street lamp, in a snowy wood. But I felt the humour might not translate. She withdrew from the wardrobe. She didn't even comment on how prettily it was decorated. 'Zis is all the space for my clothe-ses?' Then she gave me a coy smile. 'Pleez, you are joking me, *n'est-ce pas*? *Tu rigoles?*'

No, I was not *rigoles*-ing, whatever that was, but I was wishing I was. (I looked it up later. It means joking.)

'And where is my bathroom?' She was looking around desperately now. She pressed her hands flat against the walls for the imaginary door to her en-suite.

Something told me she wasn't going to like my answer.

Psychic powers at work again.

'*Viens avec moi*,' I mumbled and took her down the hall. I opened the door. Honestly, from the look on her face I thought she was going to have a heart attack, but she pulled herself together.

'*Mais*, you must take your . . .' she waved at the one tiny shelf I had allowed myself for my stuff, 'your *articles de toilette* away. There is not enough room 'ere.'

'Er, no, we are sharing.'

'*Cher*-ring? What eez *cher*-ring?'

Not something you'd know anything about, I thought almost feeling quite annoyed. But then I stopped myself. It wasn't her fault. She'd never had to '*cher*' anything before.

'We *both* use this bathroom, you,' (I pointed) 'and me.'

Back to hand on chest and palpitations.

'*Pas possible!*'

Well, yes, very possible actually. And that's not all. I was dreading this bit.

'*And* my little brother, er . . . *et mon petit frère*.'

'*Un garçon?*' She started to count on her beautifully manicured fingers, '*Un, deux, trois personnes?* I never have this in my life. Repeat to me. Three persons in one bathroom?'

No problem with her maths then.

You're upset *now*, I thought, and you haven't even met Ned.

'I ask your brother to move 'is things.' She waved her hand at Ned's carefully selected pile of skateboard mags.

'Sure.' I smiled nervously. 'You do that.'

Note to self: must speak to Ned before she does.

CHLOE'S TIP •

If you are long-waisted, your long torso can be made to seem shorter by layering. This automatically makes your legs look longer as well. Make sure the layers are made of thin fabrics – you don't want to end up waddling round like a Sumo wrestler.

Chapter 8

Sunday 9.00 p.m.

Rani rang. 'So what did Ned say, then?'

'Well, you know I've been all worried for some time about the negative attitude that Dad and Ned have been taking towards Marie-Camille, due to the excessive cleaning, etc.'

'Yes. What's that name Ned gave her again?'

'The Bag-ette.'

Rani snorted. 'That *is* quite funny.'

'For Ned, granted. Anyway, they arrived back from PC World. Marie-Camille was still unpacking upstairs and so I hinted very gently to Ned that she may ask him to move the last of his stuff . . .'

'From the bathroom?'

'From the bathroom. Ned went mental and yelled "I never asked her to come . . . she's not my bloody exchange," etc, etc, and Dad started grumbling, "Who is this girl, flippin' royalty?" and I'm all hysterical because I think if she overhears, this is not going to be good for helping her to settle in, and why can't Ned just make an effort to help me out just *once* in his life . . .'

'And then?'

'And then she walks into the kitchen: Miss Cool, all showered and changed into white designer jeans so trendy I've never heard of them and a cream halter-neck top. And, I suspect, *no bra.*'

'No!'

'Yes indeedy. Dad said hello and wasn't too hearty or

embarrassing but Ned went puce and lost the power of speech. So when she brought up the bathroom issue, Ned's nodding his head up and down like a nodding dog in the back of a car.'

'Still, that's good isn't it? You wanted them to like her.'

'I did. I did. Er, I'm just surprised it's quite soooo much. Ned's like her adoring slave now. I'm telling you, Rani, it's weird and disturbing to see him like that. It's not natural.'

'You think she's a total snooty-faced pain, don't you?'

'I do not!'

'I know you, Carrie; your psychic bonding has failed you. Go on, you can admit it to me. I won't judge you . . .'

'There's nothing to admit. No! Honestly, she is so cool. I've just been in her room. You should see her clothes. Every item packed for her, wrapped in tissue paper and dry-clean only. And she hasn't even been able to unpack it all because there's no space to put any more stuff. She's had to put loads of her clothes in my room and the bathroom looks like the most expensive chemist's you've ever been into. She's got that seaweed cream that costs about a million pounds a pot. And her life in Paris is amazing, her parents lead this really jet-set —'

'But do you like her?'

Rani has this annoying tendency to ask difficult questions.

'Of course, it's just that she's from a different world and it's taking her a while to adjust, that's all.'

Time to change the subject.

'What's Cécile like?'

'She's the most perfect girl in the world. Mum and Dad are positively drooling. Even big bro Norman can manage to be in the same room as her without hyperventilating. She is so polite and charming. She said Mum must sing some of tunes from *My Fair Lady* to her. That's how mad it is. We have heard about her many accomplishments and now I am afraid that little old self-defence classes are not shaping up very well against her instruments – clarinet, violin and piano, her dance – ballet and jazz, and her drama – classical and modern. She's top in absolutely everything in school as well.'

'Well, so are you.'

'Not *everything*. Not just maths and science and stuff. I mean, I told her I was hopeless at art and hated competitive sports and she looked at me like I was *très, très* weird. She says in her family they say being second is being nowhere.'

'Ooh. Bit heavy.'

'Exactly. And you know what my dad's like. He secretly agrees.'

'But you're the perfect daughter – you work really hard and you do come first in nearly everything. He's hardly got anything to complain about.'

'I know, but I'm loud and opinionated and tactless . . . Cécile is just so composed . . . so *perfect*.'

'Well, not to me she's not. I like you loud and opinionated and tactless.'

'Aaah. Thank you for that, Carrie.' She sighed. 'I wonder how it's all going to work out?'

'Mmm,' I said looking out at the growing pile of empty suitcases on the landing. 'I wonder.'

 **MADDY'S TIP** • • • • • • • • • • • • • • • • •

For us bra-wearing girls, getting properly fitted is really important. Especially if you are still growing, you may need new ones
quite frequently. As soon as you see a bulge of overspill coming
out of the top or sides, it's time to go and get re-fitted. I'm
about as crazy about this as going to the dentist for a filling,
but it is not as uncomfortable as boys looking at your wobbling
frontage and being puzzled by your weird shape.

Chapter 9

Monday 8.15 a.m.

On the bus. A light drizzle outside.

French girls' first day at our school. We are giving them a welcome party tonight which will be their one and only chance to socialise with the rest of the year and that means the boys as well. Under strict supervision. Mr Goodge, the chemistry teacher, Ned's form teacher and leader of the local scout troop, is doing the disco. He is Madame Debas's husband. (She kept her maiden name in order not to lose her continental aura.) It will have a French theme. It is from six-thirty to nine-thirty p.m.

I need say no more.

None of this is going to improve Marie-Camille's mood. She was already annoyed because a Year Seven mucking around at the bus stop had splashed her white jeans and cream suede pumps. I tried to make sympathetic noises but if I was honest, I was still struggling to get over her response to seeing me in my school uniform earlier this morning. We all know it is a startling shade of red but there was no need for that sort of over-reaction. Anyone would have thought an atomic bomb had gone off in the kitchen when I appeared – all that raising her hands in front of her face, like she thought she might be blinded from the glare or something. It was frankly unnecessary. However, when I saw how the French girls checked each other out this morning, I felt glad I didn't have to think about competing with clothes *every* day like Marie-Camille and her friends clearly did. It did give them a distinct advantage in the boy-magnet department, though. I noticed at the Pitsford bus stop that Wayne Brennan and his mates had come out on their motorbikes to have a look as well. His brother, Doug, must have spread the word. Every male on the bus had their eyes out on stalks. Even Sasha Dooley, über-boy-magnet of our year, didn't get much of a look-in this morning.

I had introduced Rani to Marie-Camille at the bus stop.

'This is Rani. She's one of my best friends.'

Marie-Camille turned from talking to Cécile. She had fallen upon her at the bus stop as a person on a desert island might greet a rescue party coming over the waves.

She looked Rani up and down.

Rani wants me to note that Marie-Camille's head went to one side in a puzzled way. Like she couldn't quite see the point of her. But Rani has taken against Marie-Camille. She does this sometimes with people.

'You have done good *maquillage*, er, make-up. I see zis.'

Rani's expression softened.

'Because it is hard to do good make-up wiz ze cheap products. Is it not? Bravo.'

Rani's mouth dropped open. Could be this sort of thing that is fuelling Rani's prejudice. Who knows? Marie-Camille didn't notice anyway. I don't think she meant to be tactless, it's just she's not used to our way of life yet. The bus to Boughton is a far cry from being chauffeured to school via the Eiffel Tower.

She went straight to the back with Cécile. Cécile was really friendly when Rani introduced us, and hard not to like. I could see it could be tough living with perfection though. She was also dressed expensively and elegantly in black jeans, gold chain belt and black silk sweater. I couldn't help noticing her gorgeous charm-bracelet. Gold is obviously so in this year in Paris.

They were all sitting on the back seats staring out of the window at Wayne Brennan and his mates on their motorbikes, following the coach. And giggling and waving a lot. I thought they were supposed to be sophisticated, but apparently Doug had told them that they played in a band. For once they seemed impressed about something. If only they knew the truth. Wayne's band is a scruffy group of no-hopers. Once in a blue moon, the owner of a grotty local pub lets them play, out of pity – also, since Wayne turned eighteen, he and his mates are good customers.

Jet had just twisted her head round and gave me a long look.

'Sleep late this morning?'

'No, why?'

'No reason, just couldn't help noticing that your French girl obviously spent a bit more time getting ready than you did.'

I gave that remark the cold, mirthless smirk it deserved. Fat chance of a beauty routine this morning. Marie-Camille was in the bathroom for ever. How am I meant to raise my beauty standards when I have no money for expensive products and no en-suite bathroom of my own? It is so unfair that I have been born into poverty.

She used all the hot water as well. Ned doesn't care – he never washes anyway – but it meant I had to have a tepid shower and had no time to blow dry my hair and I looked just crap. Then not a moment to even put a lick of mascara on.

Just as well Jack is away. She may be beautiful and cool but perhaps not always thinking about other people may be a tiny flaw she has.

AND READING PEOPLE'S PRIVATE DIARIES MIGHT BE A TINY FLAW YOU HAVE, RANI. READ YOUR BOOK.

AND GET THAT SMUG LOOK OFF YOUR FACE.

8.30 a.m.

The coach driver has just stopped the bus. Why? Gang of French girls caught smoking at the back. I see Marie-Camille is among their number.

5.00 p.m.

Am sitting on my bed waiting to get into the bathroom for the second time today. I want to get ready for the welcome party. Even though I know it will be a cringe-worthy event, I still want to be at least clean and out of school uniform. But I am in a good mood in spite of the wait.

And this is why: Mum's hints that the project with the French girls would be exciting actually proved to be true.

Mrs McGuy greeted us all in the form room with her customary warmth and charm. When she saw the French girls, her legendary nostrils went out on super-flare. Best bit was when she leaned forward to ask a pretty blonde girl where her teacher was. Mam'selle Nanty laughed. 'But I *am* the teacher!' Mrs McGuy reared backwards, unimpressed. She is not the sort of woman who thinks tight white trousers and wedge heels have a place in the classroom. It was bad enough when Miss Gooding tried to get away with a crop top after her clubbing holiday in Aya Napa.

Marie-Camille and her smoking crew returned from their chat

with Madame Debas looking considerably less pleased with themselves. Everybody without exchanges left for normal lessons. Did I see Doug Brennan say something to Marie-Camille on his way out? Surely not.

Only had time for brief chat with Chloe who said Agathe was lovely but very shy. Today Agathe was in a baggy, faded grey T-shirt and a knee-length navy skirt. I did a double take – yes, she *was* wearing navy pop-socks with her black lace-ups. I looked at Chloe, but her face betrayed no emotion.

Marie-Camille was staring around our form room and pulling a face. It's a shame she has to spend so much of her time looking sulky because she *is* very pretty. However I don't blame her. Our school must be a dump compared to theirs. I bet their school looks like a French version of Buckingham Palace. We are lino and peeling paint. They will be oak panelling and marble pillars.

Mrs McGuy did one of her laser-stares to calm everything down and we all went quiet. Mrs Crowe scurried in panting. Mrs McG gave her a disapproving sneer and gestured that she had the floor.

She stepped forward and told us the big news.

We're going to put on a fashion show!

5.45 p.m.

Had to pause to clear up the tea spilled on my diary. I think it was the excitement of writing those last words. I then had to dash for the shower as the bathroom was miraculously free.

'You'll be put in teams,' Mrs Crowe trilled. 'Four girls in each team. The idea is to design and make a dress that will be modelled in a fashion show at the end of the French girls' visit. We know that doesn't give you much time so we are looking for orginality and style rather than perfect stitching.'

I am relieved about this.

Mam'selle was furiously translating and all the French girls were looking very perky at this idea. Even Marie-Camille, who rattled off a question in French at Mam'selle who then turned to Mrs Crowe.

'What material will they be using and do they, er, get to choose who is in their team?'

'Black and white material and basic patterns have been provided for those that want to use them and no, the teams have been chosen already – they must have English *and* French girls in, or there really isn't much point language-wise is there?'

They said someone famous would be the judge and I wondered if they were going to ask Maddy's dad to do it. She tends not to tell people about him because then they are surprised that she isn't ultra-glamorous and wearing designer outfits every day. Like all of us, she hates her school uniform and so she still wears it like a pile of sacks. She doesn't care. She knows she can look wonderful if she feels like it, like she did at the school fund-raising dance, but to be truthful, most of the time she'd rather forget about clothes and make-up and take photos. She had politely refused any offers of make-over help, as, I suspected, had Jennifer's exchange Katia, who was *still* happily in her dungarees.

The French girls then went off to get their coach for their first day excursion – local stately home today.

6.00 p.m.
Just got time to get this down. Mum is yelling, we're going in five minutes.

On the bus home Cécile wanted to sit with Rani to discuss the project. Cécile is taking it very seriously. Marie-Camille took the seat next to me. She smiled. 'So, Wayne is big star in England.'

And I just found myself thinking that it would be a shame, just as she was feeling there was something cool about where we lived, not to let her carry on thinking it.

'Yeah, he's really famous in England,' I said.

I glanced over at Maddy across the aisle but she was listening to her iPod.

'Yeah, plays at all the big venues, Wembley, Milton Keynes . . .'

'I would like to see him play. Does he know other famous stars?'

'He knows everyone.'

She frowned. 'Why he only ride motorbike, and live 'ere?' She looked out of the window at the passing trees and pulled a face.

'Er, he likes to keep it real. You know, keep in touch with his roots.'

I thought it was time to change the subject. I spotted her drawings in the sketchbook on her lap. 'Do you have lots of ideas?' I asked her politely.

'But of course,' she replied, starting to scribble on it.

I tried again. 'What sort of thing?'

She put her pencil down and gave me a pitying look. 'I could try to explain but truly I zink I do nuzzing zat you understand. It's French fashion I do 'ere.'

'Oh, right.' I perservered. 'Well, shall I tell you about mine?' (OK, I admit – I had no ideas, but that wasn't the point.)

She gently patted my forearm, smiled sweetly and said firmly, 'No. I zink zis will not be interesting for me. I hope you understand zis.'

A lesser person might have found this dispiriting.

'But we're on the same team,' I bleated.

'I know! So wonderful zat my mother teach me so much. Take me to all the best designers in Paris, *n'est-ce pas*? I will do good design for us.'

'What makes you so sure that your design will be the best?' Maddy had taken off her headphones and leaned across to look directly at Marie-Camille.

'And you are?' Marie-Camille responded, giving her a quick up and down glance.

I knew Maddy sensed style-wise she had just been firmly dismissed.

'My name's Maddy.'

'And you 'ave a design for the competition? I do not see you in the art room today.'

'I'm going to be taking the photos. I like photography and Mrs Crowe has given me permission to take pictures of the dresses and the show. I'm not doing a design myself. I do Spanish.'

Marie-Camille nodded as if this explained a great deal.

'You see, Maddy,' she said, smiling sympathetically at her, 'if you 'ave a parent who is very famous in ze world of fashion like mine . . .'

I caught Maddy's eye and grinned.

'. . . you just know some zings. Zey are in your blood. If you not 'ave zis experience, I cannot explain . . .'

And you could see she felt Maddy was the very last person on earth who would know anything about it.

Maddy nodded sagely. 'Maybe you're right.'

Got to go now. Mr Goodge's mellow grooves await me.

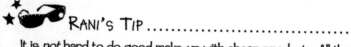

RANI'S TIP ....

It is *not* hard to do good make-up with cheap products. All the supermarkets have excellent make-up and skin-care ranges now. You can get up-to-the-minute goodies and can afford to change your look with the season's latest products. This is instead of feeling sick of wearing the weird-coloured Chanel lipstick that cost you a small fortune and is now *so* last year.

Chapter 10

On bus. Could not find my hair straighteners this morning. Annoyed at this and due to lack of sleep last night thanks to antics of Marie-Camille. Went to search downstairs and saw she had managed to stagger down and crawl on to a stool. In spite of the make-up she still looked very peaky. Mum asked her if she was coming down with the bug that was going round. As soon as Mum turned her back she shot me a glance of pure rage. I don't feel I am *totally* to blame. Ned was chatting away to her as if nothing had happened. He appeared to have a piece of flattened road-kill flopping up and down over his forehead. The question about the missing tongs had been answered. I opened my mouth to comment but Mum shot me a 'do-not-be-mean-to-Ned' glare. On another day I would have said something anyway, but Ned was spared due to the fact that:

a) I was in a rush.

b) I was sort of grateful to him for not sneaking about last night to Mum.

Normal service will be resumed shortly.

By the way, Dr Jennings, I hear your voice of disapproval – why would I want to say something mocking and possibly unkind to my little brother? I will tell you why – revenge. It is not nice to just *once* wear a pair of unflattering shorts and be known as 'fat-arse' for months afterwards, you know. It takes more than one evening to mend those sort of scars.

Stop laughing, Rani.

I may have resigned myself to the fact you are incapable of respecting my privacy when it comes to my diary, but please refrain from making light of my pain.

5.30 p.m.

Supposed to be doing some homework.

So – last night.

I'm not sure what Marie-Camille was expecting but Mr Goodge, dressed in a stripy jumper and beret leaping about behind two speakers, was surely not it. Nor were the plastic flags hung about the classroom, and curling sandwiches. And she'd already seen what the boys were like. But she remained in a very perky mood.

She had arrived in suspiciously baggy sweater and jeans. As had Manon and Océane, her two best friends. Two minutes after arriving, they dashed into the toilets. Marie-Camille reappeared in silver shorts and a black lace top. She *was* wearing a bra this time. You could see it clearly through her flimsy shirt.

Madame Debas was beside herself but she could hardly phone all the parents and ask them to come back straight away.

'Marie-Camille seems very cheerful,' Chloe observed. Chloe was looking cool as always in white cotton dress and ballet pumps. Marie-Camille had not been exactly friendly towards her so far. Chloe has this effect on girls who think that they are pretty gorgeous. Chloe is just effortlessly simply *more* gorgeous. So let's just say Marie-Camille hadn't made a big effort to be chummy. The French girls mostly looked like they were going to be on the cover of *Vogue*. Except for Katia, who had made an effort and was out of her old dungarees and in a new, almost identical, pair. And Agathe, of course. Not many people would team a check shirt with a bold floral pinafore dress, apart from my mum, but there you go.

'Something's up,' Rani said, coming over to us. 'Those girls are planning something. Cécile was on her mobile for ages after school but I think from her tone that she's backed out of whatever they've got up their sleeves.' She looked over at Cécile talking to Agathe by the door.

'Look, while we've got a moment, I really want to talk to you about something. I'm seriously worried. It's about my dad feeling I should do loads of extra-curricular stuff; I think he's going to make me – oops! Watch out, Marie-Camille's coming over. Smiling? What can this mean? Act casual everybody.'

But she needn't have taken that tone because Marie-Camille was in a great mood.

'Carrie,' she gushed. She gave Rani and Chloe a brief nod. 'Come to speak wiz us. Over 'ere.' She pointed to Manon and Océane.

'Well, er, OK.' I couldn't believe it. She actually wanted me to hang out with her friends.

I saw Rani's face fall. 'Oh, sorry, I know you wanted to talk . . .' I winced.

'No, go on, it's OK. I'll tell you another time.'

So I went over with Marie-Camille who was really friendly and interested in my life. They did ask some rather uncomfortable questions about Wayne and his friends but I thought I fended them off well. And then they asked lots of silly things like what time everyone went to bed in England and stuff. I was pleased because it meant that she might be starting to think we weren't that sad in spite of the fact that Mr Goodge was enthusiastically playing 'The Birdie Song' and doing all the actions.

Talk about being lulled into a false sense of security.

The welcome evening passed without incident, we even danced a bit with the boys and it wasn't too bad. She was even nice to Doug. I couldn't help noticing that she spent a lot longer in the toilets than the average girl. I suspect she was smoking. I think I caught a whiff of it on her, but when I went in I couldn't smell smoke but the windows had been opened wide – you could hear the traffic outside.

It was only when we got home and I'd been in bed for a while that I heard a familiar sound outside our house. I got up. The traffic noise that I had heard earlier was Wayne Brennan's bike, which I could now see from my window – he was driving up and down our road. I shut it firmly and tried to get to sleep. I heard a bang, slam, of the window in the next room – obviously Marie-Camille shutting out the noise as well. Oh, that I could have been so naïve, so foolish. It can be a curse always to think the best of people.

I was woken from the land of nod by small stones rattling against my window. I looked at my clock. It was 1.23 a.m.

'Carrieeee. Carrieeee.'

I went to open it. Outside I could see Marie-Camille weaving around across the grass, twirling a cigarette in one hand.

'What the hell are you doing down there?' I hissed.

She put a finger to her lips and made shushing noises.

'You 'elp me. I must to get in my bed.'

'Where have you *been*?'

'Where 'ave I been? WHERE 'AVE I BEEN? I 'ave been in ze town. I 'ave 'orrible time. Zis is not good town. Bad, bad Middleton.'

I could hear Wayne's bike disappearing down the road.

'Oh no! You sneaked out to go out with Wayne and his friends! *Why* did you do that?'

'WHY?! You ask me *why* Carrie?'

I wish I hadn't asked why because she took a step back and shook one of her feeble fists at me. She then promptly fell over, losing her cigarette in the flowerbed. I watched it go out. She staggered towards the drainpipe and began to climb, muttering darkly. Somehow, with me risking my life leaning out to grab her, she made it up to my window. I dragged her in like a sack of coal over the sill.

She managed to crawl over to my bed and clamber aboard.

'No,' I whispered. 'Not here, this is my room.'

She waved a hand airily around her face.

'I sleep 'ere.' Her eyes wandered unsteadily around her. Then they anchored on me. This seemed to energise her briefly.

'You, YOU,' she said, pointing an accusing finger. 'You say Wayne is big rock star. Your friend Wayne, 'e say 'e is big rock star and we go to see him play in town. I go. BUT YOU LIE!'

I appreciated her emotions were obviously stirred but I was scared Mum and Dad would hear.

'Shhhh.'

'No shush-shush *me*, Carrie. YOU LIE! Wayne Brennan is NOT big rock star. 'E play in little room in 'orrible pub called Ze Duck Which Need A Bath or somezing like zis. Really, zis is not a nice place.'

So she had been to The Dirty Duck. What a dump that was. A far cry from the clubs of the Champs Élysées.

'I never speak wiz zis person or 'is stupid friends again.' She wagged her finger in my direction. 'I never . . .' Her head lolled over to one side and her eyes closed. 'I never . . .'

She had to be moved. I wanted my bed back. After a couple of tentative prods I realised more vigorous measures were going to be needed. I leaned over her, got my arms under hers and tried to haul her up.

'Come on, Marie-Camille – wake up.'

I got her torso up. Her head lolled on my shoulder.

'Don't want to disturb anything sis, but what are you doing?'

Ned was standing at the door of my room looking curiously at the scene.

I gave Marie-Camille a heave. She flopped further forward and started drooling on to my neck. Eurghh!

'Get over here, Ned. And be quiet.'

'Are you sure?' He held up both hands. 'I don't want to intrude on anything private. You know I'm cool with every-one doing their own thing though, honestly, I have to admit I am a trifle shocked. But it just goes to show you never can tell . . .'

'Shut up, Ned, and help me. This is not the time for your so-called humour. She's over-tired and she's been drinking with Wayne Brennan and his mates. I want to wake her up and I need you to help me get her to her own bed.'

'Thank the Lord. I was dreading having to tell Jack you were lesbotic.' Ned leaped towards Marie-Camille with frankly too much enthusiasm.

'OK,' I said firmly. 'I'm going to try and stand her up. Get ready to steady her . . .'

But as soon as I tried she flopped back on to the bed. Her eyes opened wide. 'YOU LIE,' she shouted before falling back asleep. We were back where we started.

'This is no use. She'll have to sleep here. I'll go to her room.'

Ned looked disappointed. 'You sure? If I could just get my arms around her . . .'

'No, you weirdo. Leave her alone.'

'Oh, *I'm* the weirdo, am I? My lips are sealed Carrie, but I know what I saw.'

'Shut up, you sad moron, and let's go. She's zonked out now.'

He was looking at her with a soppy look on his face.

'Come on, you,' I said and pushed him out of the door.

And then I got no sleep. I couldn't help feeling partly to blame for the whole thing. Why had I said all that rubbish about Wayne? Then I had to get up really early to swap beds so Mum and Dad wouldn't be suspicious and she was pretty grumpy about it.

I had hoped she might have calmed down by the morning. But nooooo. *I* am personally responsible for the whole evening. It is *my* awful friends, *my* awful town and *my* awful country, which seem to be the problem. I did point out that if she'd only told me what she was planning I could have told her it would be a disaster, but that didn't seem to be a valid point as far as she was concerned.

'What I don't understand, Carrie . . .' Rani sighed later, 'is why on earth you told her that rubbish about Wayne in the first place?'

We were with Chloe by the lockers at home time.

'I don't know. It was stupid. I just saw that they were impressed that Wayne was in a band and then I thought they would think it was cool if I sort of *exaggerated* it a bit.'

Chloe and Rani gave me a look.

'And that they wouldn't think where we lived was so lame,' I ended feebly.

'So you're ashamed of where we live?'

I squirmed. Rani should be an interrogator for the army.

'Look, it was a stupid thing to say, I know that now. She hates me. Manon hates me. Océane hates me. And so do Melanie and Sasha who had also had to contend with sneaking them into *their* houses in the middle of the night. I FEEL AWFUL.'

'Honestly,' Rani said with a sigh. 'I don't sit next to you on the bus for *one* day, *one day*, and this happens. From now on you are *expressly* forbidden from sitting without me. God knows what you'll say next. Brad Pitt lives down your road? Your mum is about to go on tour with Madonna?'

'OK, Rani, that's enough. Look, don't feel too terrible,' Chloe said kindly. 'You told a silly lie but you couldn't possibly have guessed what the consequences would be. How could creeping out of the house be all your fault? They have to be responsible for their own actions. And what if anything had happened to them? It was a totally crazy thing to do.'

'They say they won't do it again . . .'

'Yeah, but only because they didn't have a good time,' Rani snorted. 'They didn't care about the danger they put themselves into. Or think about the families who are looking after them.'

'Agathe told me that Marie-Camille sneaks out a lot in Paris. She meets up with Manon and Océane sometimes. Her parents are hardly ever at home and so she goes out when the house-keeper has gone to bed,' Chloe added.

'Wow, that must be pretty cool.' I sighed. 'Better than living in the concentration camp that is my house, with Mum and Dad practically in watchtowers with spotlights trained on me at all times.'

'Well, they didn't see Marie-Camille climb back in so you were lucky,' Rani snapped. She *was* in one of her aggressive moods.

'I madly thought that helping her get back in and making sure Mum and Dad didn't find out might have brought us closer,' I mused sadly.

'I thought Ned said it did,' Chloe sniggered.

I gave her a withering look. 'Oh tee-hee-hee. Seriously, I thought that she would be grateful I helped her.'

'Carrie,' Rani said seriously. 'Chloe and I have discussed this and we have decided that you have got to stop thinking that being rich is an excuse for really selfish behaviour. She's not special, she's not kind and she's a horrible snob. She used you. She got all that information out of you at the party so she knew when it would be safe to get Wayne to collect her.'

Ouch. That hurt.

Chloe continued. 'Rani does have a point, Carrie. She won't speak to Agathe because she's a scholarship girl. Or to Susie's exchange, Fleur, because she has a free place as her mum is the school nurse. This morning she didn't even try to hide her disappointment that she wasn't in the same design group as Cécile or the others.'

I couldn't deny the truth of this. Cécile and Rani were with Chloe and Agathe. Marie-Camille and I had been put with Fleur and Susie. If there was an Olympic event for sulky pouting, she'd have been in with a chance of the gold medal.

'How was she today? With the dress designs?' Rani asked.

Our design meeting had been rather tense. We had all shown our drawings and Marie-Camille had not even bothered to look at anyone else's.

'Er. I told you. We haven't *quite* resolved it.'

'And why not?'

'Well, Susie's design was a big meringue and mine was a stick lady with a triangle.'

'That's because you've been concentrating on the catwalk and set design, isn't it? I looked at your drawings. Putting the huge red and magenta banners against the stark black and white of the stage is going to make a wonderful bold statement,' said Chloe.

'Thank you,' I said, blushing. I was excited about it. 'My dress design was never going to count. But Fleur had done a very simple halter-neck dress that Susie and I thought had some good elements.'

'Mmm, and Marie-Camille?' prompted Rani.

'She felt that with her vast experience of the fashion world – due to her mother being a style icon – that her dress would have the most to offer.'

'She refused to consider Fleur's at all, didn't she?'

'Well, she just felt that Fleur might not have the same understanding as she did and that the judges would need to see more of an expert . . .'

'So you all had a big argument,' Rani said gleefully.

'No, we didn't. We just found it hard to come to an agreement.'

To be honest it would have been so much easier to just let Marie-Camille have her way but there was something about the way she spoke to Fleur and how she tore our designs apart that made Susie and me determined not to give in – famous mother or no famous mother. The session had ended with the final decision that we would use elements of both. Marie-Camille was pretty mad about it, but at least she had agreed.

'Cécile was lovely about being with Agathe and really friendly. She seemed positively delighted,' Chloe said admiringly.

'Time to face up to the fact that the Paris Princess is not your French kindred spirit, I think,' Rani said bluntly.

Mmm, I know she had behaved badly last night but it *was* pretty much my fault. And she *had* agreed to compromise on the dress design. I felt that was a huge breakthrough.

I cannot help my dogged and optimistic nature, so in spite of everything that's happened – give up? Not quite yet.

★ CARRIE'S TIP • • • • • • • • • • • • • • • •

If you think you have shapeless ankles, avoid shoes with ankle straps. These will emphasise the exact part you don't like and, if you are really unlucky, make your lower legs resemble a bit of beef brisket rolled up and ready for the oven. Keep straps on shoes below this danger zone.

Chapter 11

Wednesday 12.20 p.m.

OK. Now. Now is the time to give up.

Got to school and noticed that Marie-Camille had disappeared between the bus and the classroom. She had been very quiet since we got home yesterday. A state of affairs that Doug Brennan could only envy. Although it was all in French, safe to say we all got the drift of her little chat with *him* on the bus this morning. A Year Seven came into our classroom first thing with a note. Mrs McGuy read it and said that Mrs Crowe wanted to see me, Susie and Fleur in her office before first session. We were all equally baffled as we climbed the stairs. Mrs Crowe and Mam'selle Nanty were standing by the desk and looked grave. Marie-Camille was standing next to them, I gave her a searching look but her face was expressionless. Mrs Crowe twisted the large ring on her finger, took a deep breath and began.

'Er, I am very sorry to have to have this talk with you, but after Marie-Camille had spoken to me this morning, I really felt I had no option.'

Susie and I gave each other confused looks. What was she talking about?

'She came to me extremely upset this morning. *Extremely* upset about yesterday's dress-making session.'

I opened my mouth to say 'What?' but Mrs Crowe swept on.

'This project is supposed to be a joint project, a project where everyone gets a chance to contribute.'

Time for us to look at Marie-Camille, now. In her big brown eyes there lay an expression I could only describe as concern mixed with disappointment.

'She has told me that in spite of her very best efforts, she found it very difficult to get anyone to listen to her.'

Mam'selle Nanty tut-tutted and shook her head. Our mouths were opening and closing like little goldfish in a bowl now.

'How unfriendly to our French visitor, Susie and Carrie, to refuse to consider her design – I think that she actually found you both very intimidating.' (Marie-Camille nodded gravely.) 'She tells me you got very angry with her but she had not been able to understand because you were both talking too fast. *Not* very considerate of you. You must understand that she is new to this country and couldn't be expected to understand everything.'

More nodding from Mam'selle.

'But all we said was —' Susan protested.

Mrs Crowe held up her hand. 'Did you or did you not refuse to consider Marie-Camille's design?'

'No!' I gasped. '*She* refused to consider anyone else's —'

Marie-Camille's big brown eyes widened. She took Mrs Crowe's sleeve. Mrs C turned to her.

'Do you have something to say, Marie-Camille?'

Marie-Camille looked very, very hurt. 'Carrie 'as made mistake. Zat is not true; I look at Fleurs's design for a long, long time. I speak to Fleur, I discuss wiz Fleur 'er drawing. About every zing in 'er drawing.'

It could not be denied that she had held up her design and told us all in no uncertain terms what was wrong with it.

Mrs Crowe turned to Susie and me. 'Is this true? It sounds like

Marie-Camille was far from ignoring other people's work . . . Did she discuss your dress, Fleur?'

Fleur hung her head and nodded.

'And she looked at your designs, Susie?' Mrs Crowe swept on.

'Yes, but she didn't —' Susie blurted.

'Did Marie-Camille look carefully at everyone's designs?' Mrs C snapped. 'Yes or no?'

I could have said she didn't look at mine very carefully but thinking of my stick lady decided to let it go. I couldn't let it end there though.

'Look,' I cried, 'yes, she did look at Susie and Fleur's designs but only to say —'

'Enough!' Mrs Crowe put up her hand. 'That is enough. I am very disappointed. I think the best way to make amends for trying to exclude Marie-Camille would be for you all to agree to start again today, working *together* . . .'

I gave a sigh of relief. 'But that's *exactly* what we wanted . . .'

'. . . on Marie-Camille's design.'

'On *Marie-Camille's* design?' Susie wailed.

Mrs Crowe retaliated, 'Do you have a problem with that Susie? Carrie? Fleur?'

Resistance was futile. We hung our heads and murmured agreement. Marie-Camille beamed.

We left the room.

She gazed happily at us. 'Zat is better now, Carrie, *non*? I zay nuzzing to you last night because I zink it better I speak to teacher first about your little problem. But now we are understanding each uzzer. We start again. And now we can all be friends, *n'est-ce pas*?' she said firmly. 'I am prepared to forget zat you tell me BIG

LIE. I forget zat you let me go out wiz zis 'orrible boy who is not a rock star, Wayne Brennan. I forget zat you know little about style 'ere in Boughton and so not understand why my dress is best. We make a new start. I will get my drawings. We start work *immédiatement.*'

We trudged after her into the art room like the chain gang we were.

Spoke to Rani and Chloe at break.

'Have I been a total prat about Marie-Camille?' I asked them.

'If you call thinking that being,

a) snobbish,

b) reckless,

c) selfish, and

d) arrogant, are cool – then yes. Perhaps a bit.'

Rani is nothing if not honest. But I deserved it.

'I'm so sorry, Rani, about the dance. You were right, she was only using me to get information about when it would be safe to sneak out of my house. And I knew you wanted to talk about your dad.'

'Yeah,' Rani nodded. 'But don't worry, I'll be in so many after-school clubs soon that you won't be seeing me much anyway.'

'Rani! Don't say that.'

'It's true. He wants to start me with extra maths.'

'Oh God,' I said. 'Rosie Stevens will make you one of her *I'm totally MENTAL about MATHS* badges.'

'Still, better than Mr Grant's History Alive! group,' Chloe comforted.

We all knew what that meant. A lot of running around the playing field in rough linen with Jackie Watkins and Sarah Li, wielding pikestaffs.

'I'm so, so sorry. I let myself get a bit dazzled by all that Paris Princess stuff.'

'To be fair, Carrie *was* only trying to see the best in her,' Chloe said supportively. 'And I'm sure there *are* nice things about Marie-Camille.'

There was a pause.

I broke the silence. 'I'm sure there are. And so what if she thinks our lives are small and crappy? I'm going back to being happy with my crappy, small life.'

'And your crappy, small friends,' Rani said opening her arms for a hug. Chloe, Rani and me then had a big hug-in. Just as Ned walked past.

'At it again, sis?' He raised his eyebrows.

'And your crappy, small brother,' Chloe yelled after him.

8.30 p.m.

So, a day that started so badly did get better. And I got a card from Jack.

Dear Carrie,

It's a hard life here in the mountains. We are forced out once a day to clamber around the mountain in the sleeting rain. I hope that the webbed fingers I'll have by the time I get back won't put you off. Mum is only keeping from going mad with gin and day-time telly. She swears she will never venture out of the city again. We are totally isolated so I am a lonely man living amongst the rocky crags without you and with only Tom's sweaty socks for company. Tom fell down a pothole on one of our rambles and had to be manhandled out by me and a guy passing on a tractor, but only his pride is hurt. I feel obliged to let you know that a couple of girls have been hanging around our cottage and have been pestering us outrageously. We go out every so often and shout at them to go away. They run off for a while but always come back. Tom went out to have a word with their mother but she just baa-ed and carried on eating the grass. It's so harsh there's no mobile phone reception here either. Can't wait to see you when I get back. How are those French girls behaving? Hope they live up to expectations.

Love, Jack xx

8.50 p.m.

Phoned Rani. Does she think 'Love, Jack' is the same as 'I love you'?

No. She doesn't.

I did know that anyway. Actually.

⭐ 🕶 CHLOE'S TIP • • • • • • • • • • • • • • • •

Black and white eveningwear is one thing; in natural daylight these colours don't suit everyone. Black and white on a lot of skin tones make you look pale and washed out. Check what colours suit you with some friends and start looking for them when you shop. You don't have to throw out your old clothes, just start to think more carefully about what colours you are going to wear near your face.

Chapter 12

Thursday 8.15 a.m.

On the bus.

I cannot speak today, Rani. I have too much to write. There have been developments on the Marie-Camille design front.

Do not disturb me.

This morning, just as we were leaving, a parcel arrived. And I mean a big one. The postman had to knock, Mum signed for it and came staggering back into the kitchen. Terrible pong in there this morning. Ned had raided Dad's aftershave. I don't know if I can take much more. Worse, Marie-Camille encourages this puppy love by actually speaking to him from time to time. Why, oh why would some mad lunatic has give him the *leading role* in the Year Seven production of *Joseph*? Has the world gone mad?

Back to the parcel.

'It's for you, Marie-Camille,' Mum said with her pretending-not-to-be-bursting-with-curiosity expression.

'Yes, I know zis, I am expecting a package.'

'What is it?' Ha. Mum cracked before I did.

'It is for the fashion show, for the dress. *Le tissu.* How do you say it? The material for the dress.'

What the hell was she on about?

'But we *have* the material for the dress,' I wailed. 'We have been sewing it *all* week.'

She can't have forgotten. The one thing we *didn't* argue about at the first meeting was the material. It was going to be black.

Then Mrs Crowe had handed us a roll and Marie-Camille had rubbed it between her fingers in disbelief. She immediately went off to ask Mrs Crowe if she was *rigoles*-ing. It looked like Cécile was having the same emotional trauma with her roll of white fabric. They had had a good indignant jabber in the middle of the art room before returning to their tables, spluttering disapproval in French. But now Marie-Camille was carefully peeling back layers of tissue and revealing yards of obviously expensive black satin.

'The *school* material?' She looked at me as if I was mad. '*Tu rigoles*.' (Here we go again.) 'A peasant would be ashamed to wear it.'

I asked what the hell we had been sewing all week, and she looked at me again, but this time as if I was mentally defective.

'Do you know nuzzing about haute couture? When you make a dress you make a *toile*, a, er, a copy of the dress made of thin material. This way everything is perfect before you *coupe*,' – she made scissor movements – 'your expensive material.'

Then, from under the satin, she started pulling out jet beads, feathers, black sequins, and silk lace trimmings.

What are you doing, Rani? Stop poking me. I told you I need to write this down.

OK, I give up. I can stand this attention-seeking behaviour no longer. This better be good. Go on then. Say what you have to say.

8.35 a.m.
Still on the bus.

Sorry, Rani, I take it all back.

Rani has just told me that Marie-Camille wasn't the only girl who got a parcel this morning. Cécile got one. Except hers was full of white satin and accessories. It's like the good and bad fairy.

She had asked her parents to send it after the first day in school. Just like Marie-Camille apparently, except Marie-Camille's housekeeper had arranged hers. I have just looked at the back of the bus and seen them both with big boxes on their laps comparing contents. How could I have missed Cécile carrying that at the bus stop? Rani says it's because I was doing my make-up. Which was true, due to lack of bathroom time. Marie-Camille had popped her head around my bedroom door this morning with a pot of her seaweed cream in her hand.

'I 'ave somezing for you,' she said.

'Wow, that's so kind . . .' I began, overwhelmed.

She produced a small tube in her other hand. 'I see zis morning zat you 'ave ze spot.' She jabbed her forehead. ''Ere. Zis is not nice. I lend you some of this ointment. Maybe it 'elp. You do not want to look, what does Ned say ze word is? A minger?'

Surely this parcel thing can't be OK? I feel confident that Mrs Crowe will not allow it. English fair play and all that.

7.30 p.m.

Mrs Crowe has allowed it.

I cannot believe it. Cécile and Marie-Camille persuaded her that if this was truly to be a cultural exchange they would like to show us peasant English *rosbifs* how real haute couture designers work. Marie-Camille also said it wasn't fair that the English girls were allowed to bring things from home for their designs, and not them. As the things English girls had brought from home so far were some large safety pins for Sasha's dress and some silver foil for Jackie's *Doctor Who* sci-fi number, I wasn't sure this argument held up. But Cécile did what Chloe would call 'a charm offensive' on everyone, and eventually Mrs Crowe caved.

Cécile was very good at this. Rani was still annoyed that her design had been chosen for the show and not Chloe's.

'Chloe's was much more fun and interesting than Cécile's,' Rani wailed. 'It really was. Totally different. Cécile's is elegant and beautiful, but I thought Chloe's was loads more exciting.'

'But Chloe did say that Cécile's design was the best. She said it was gorgeous.'

'Well, that's Chloe. Too blimmin' modest.'

'What did Agathe think?'

'She obviously thought that Chloe's idea was a bit way out. She went with Cécile straight away. She adores Cécile. I know now why Cécile was so thrilled to be on her team. Agathe's mum works as a seamstress at Dior. That was what Agathe meant by her mum being in 'cloth'. She must have taught her everything she knows because Agathe sews like a dream. However, I don't want to be harsh, but Agathe's judgement on fashion . . .' She pulled a face.

'It's not like Cécile bulldozed you into it though, is it? You discussed it all in a civilized fashion. Not like Marie-Camille.'

'True, I suppose. They do always seem to get their own way, by fair means or foul, don't they?'

This made me feel a bit uneasy. I don't know why, but I started thinking about them meeting the boys on Sunday. We are all meeting up at The Coffee Bean. They were certainly asking a lot of questions about it.

9.00 p.m.

Re-read Jack's letter. I know in my heart that I want to write this letter to him:

Dearest Jack,

I am missing you so much. I miss the way your dark hair falls over your eyes. I miss the way you smile when you see me. I miss holding your hand and I would very much like to kiss you again soon. Because it makes my legs go unsteady. I want to be sitting next to you in The Coffee Bean and leaning on your shoulder because you are the most interesting boy I have ever met: funny, kind, you listen but you make your own mind up about things. I really think that I have fallen for you in a big way. I thought I liked boys before, but it didn't feel like this. I think I love you. Do you feel the same way? (At all?)

Carrie xxx

So I did. But then I got another piece of paper and wrote:

Dear Jack,

How's it going in mountain-land? Life is pretty busy with the French girls around. Marie-Camille is like the princess in The Princess and the Pea *story. We're all busy like the birds and mice in the* Cinderella *cartoon sewing away at these dresses we are making together. Marie-Camille has hi-jacked our team, but I have to say her design is très sophisticated. Does it seem weird to hear about this when you are crouched amongst rugged crags of Wales? The time seems to be going very slowly now you are away buried in your books. We're looking forward to you getting back. Jennifer tells us she has been asking and asking Chris Jones (or 'Chris – what on earth were you thinking, Carrie', as you chose to call him) if she can come over after school and help him with his revision. Apparently he has declined this kind offer.*

Maybe he's not as thick as I thought.

Must go now. See you soon.

Love, Carrie xx

9.45 p.m.

Rani phoned. Told her about wanting to send letter revealing my true feelings. She gave a strangled cry.

'Step away from the revealing, crazy, "I love you" letter, Carrie. Step away. Have you stepped away?'

Reluctantly I put it down on the dressing table.

'Yes.'

'Pick up the letter from a normal person and not a love-crazed-stalker-type person. Have you done that?'

I had.

'Good. Now put it in the envelope.'

I did.

'Seal it so you can't change your mind and swap letters.'

I sealed it.

'Excellent. Now write what you weigh in black felt pen all over the first letter.'

'What?'

'Well, do something to stop yourself being tempted to send it again.'

I wrote my bra size in felt pen down one side.

'Thank you, Rani, you are a good friend.'

'You'd do the same for me.'

And I would.

CARRIE'S TIP ● ● ● ● ● ● ● ● ● ● ● ● ● ● ● ● ●

Customise your writing paper. Get a passport photo, put it on a sheet of white paper and photocopy it five to ten times (if you can find a colour photocopier, even better, but black and white is cool). Cut out the photos and stick one in each corner, or wherever looks good to you. Then photocopy again, as many sheets as you need. The photo can be of you, or you may want to do some with you and your friends, family, boyfriends or your pets.

Chapter 13

Friday 6.10 p.m.

French girls were at lunch today. They were in school for the afternoon to work on their 'My Visit to England' projects.

Marie-Camille put down her plate of macaroni cheese and looked around the table. 'So. Tell me about zis trip to London tomorrow. Where do we go?'

I plunged in. 'We're going first to Covent Garden. There's lots of small shops and street theatre around there.'

Marie-Camille stifled a yawn.

'And then afterwards we'll go with my mum and Rani's mum to Oxford Street.'

Marie-Camille leaned across the table. 'Chloe?'

Chloe eyed her warily. 'Yes?'

'Which shops do you go to tomorrow?'

'Oh well, TopShop, H&M ... And I know there's a shop in Bond Street which has Lucy Kell designs and she's my favourite designer.'

'Lucy Kell,' Marie-Camille sounded surprised. 'You 'ave seen her work?'

'Well, only in magazines.'

'Ah, in *magazines*.' Marie-Camille smirked at Manon and Océane. 'When I come to London wiz my mother we visit zis shop. You 'ave to make ze appointment to go zere or be veree, veree good customer. We see Lucy Kell dresses. My mother, she take me to all ze shops. She love to 'ave me wiz 'er when she shop for clothes-ses. I have such the good eye.'

Maddy went cross-eyed for a moment but Marie-Camille didn't see.

'You're very lucky,' Chloe said politely. 'I have to admit I haven't been to London that often.'

Marie-Camille shrugged. 'I see London many time.'

'I know you've been before,' Maddy said, watching her inspect a piece of macaroni as if it were a slug on the end of her fork, 'but it's different to go with a gang of friends; we'll have fun.'

She stared at Maddy. '*You* are going? You are going wiz us tomorrow?'

'Yup. Carrie's mom asked me.'

'Of course.' She nodded. 'In London zey 'ave more ze shops wiz ze larger size, *non*? You will 'ave more ze choice, *non*?'

Maddy clambered off the bench. 'Do your mouth and brain *ever* connect?' She sighed. 'I'm off to develop some photos.'

Chloe, Rani and I glared at Marie-Camille. She stared straight back and lifted her hands in the air.

'What? What?'

7.35 p.m.

Chloe phoned. She sounded in a funny mood but she said she was fine.

I got it out of her in the end.

'The thing is, Carrie, you know how much I love fashion and designing . . .'

'Yes, and you're brilliant at it.'

'But I'm not, not really. Now the French girls are here, they're just so sophisticated and they know so much more than me. They talk about shops and designers and labels – I've never heard of half of them. I know nothing compared to them. I feel like a fool. Like I've been deluding myself all this time thinking I've got any taste.'

'That's rubbish, and you know it,' I protested.

'It's not. They're always catching me out, discussing designers and asking if I know about them and I just *don't*.'

'You do! You know more than anyone.'

'Maybe *here*, Carrie. But here is a very small place compared to Paris or London. And she's got a mother who takes her to all the most exclusive shops. How can I ever compete in that world when I don't ever have a chance of going to those places?'

'Because you're clever and have more natural style in your little finger than any of those girls do in their whole designer-clad bodies. I promise you that's what counts.'

'I was so looking forward to our trip tomorrow and I know Agathe is. It's just been a bit spoiled by being turned into yet another opportunity for Marie-Camille and her friends to show us how much more *chic* and *belle* they are than us.'

'Look, Chloe, let's just be ourselves and have a good time. It doesn't matter what they think. It really doesn't.'

'Must be nice to have a famous mum who you can swan around London with shopping together though.' She sighed. 'I think my mum would like to do it if we had any money.'

'Well, that's one up on me because even if my mum was a multi-millionaire she'd still be a slave to polyester and multi-coloured prints.'

'Has Marie-Camille heard from her mum yet?'

'No, she's still travelling. You might think she'd want to check that her daughter's not staying with axe-murderers, but maybe it's better than having a mum who uses your mobile to tag you like a common criminal, like mine.'

And we both felt that in the mum stakes perhaps Marie-Camille had a winner.

I felt this all the more when mine came in while I was on the phone to Chloe, stony faced and not at all like a beautiful famous actress. She was brandishing a piece of paper.

'Apparently Rani gave this to Marie-Camille on the bus,' she said.

I wondered what she'd been scribbling.

'Rani gave it to Marie-Camille, but luckily she handed it to me; her English wasn't quite up to it.'

It had *Tips for the London Visitor* written across the top.

Mum put it on my dressing table and left the room without further comment.

I grabbed it and read it out over the phone to Chloe.

'Tips for the London Visitor.

'Although all Londoners, especially in Oxford Street appear to be in a hurry, do not be fooled. They find groups of foreign exchange students, chattering away on the street, absolutely charming. Please make sure you stand right in the middle of the pavement to ensure that they get the best possible view of this delightful sight.

'On the Underground escalators, always stand on both sides. It is fun to see the people building up behind you. Do not be alarmed. They are not angry – those cries and hand gestures are purely traditional. Whatever you do, don't let them pass you: it will cause offence.

'People on the Tube love to chat. People appearing to read

newspapers are showing the customary signal of an Englishman inviting a conversation. The convention is to pull down the paper with a sharp tug and engage in some friendly banter. See their response! Who says the English are reserved!

'When on London buses, do not think of paying with anything other than a twenty pound note. A driver will be offended to be offered anything less from a tourist. The muttering from people behind you is simply due to jealousy from Londoners who are denied this privilege and have to carry a simple travelcard. In London, a shaking fist is sign of warm farewell.

'Don't leave Oxford Street without attempting the lucky hat dash. The trick is to knock off a policeman's or traffic warden's helmet and then run with it up the street. If you can get to Marble Arch without him catching you, it is good luck for a year! Once he has got his breath back he will surely congratulate you heartily.

'The End.'

It cheered Chloe up a bit.

 RANI'S TIP •

Macaroni cheese is fine once in a while, but good hair and skin come from a good diet. Try to eat lots of fruit and veg. If you find it hard, drink smoothies to get those important beautifying vitamins down you. You can make your own with a blender. Delicious!

Chapter 14

Phoned Chloe. Feeling strangely nervous.

'What are you going to wear?' I asked.

'God. What time is it? I'm just going to wear jeans and a jacket,' she groaned.

I was not to be fooled by this.

'OK, what jeans and what jacket?'

'My skinny black jeans and my greeny tweed jacket, you know, the one I got at the second-hand shop and cropped the bottom off so its kind of tight and short. The one with the black velvet ribbon I sewed all around the bottom and cuffs.'

'Yeah and . . .?'

'A white shirt underneath.'

'And . . .?'

'My black beads and that's all, Carrie, because otherwise I'm on to my sad baggy knickers and they really are not that interesting. What are you going to be wearing?'

'My little grey jacket, dusky pink T-shirt, my grey cords and my black boots. Thank God I'm going to get some new clothes. I want something new to wear for Jack's return. I've got my birthday money and I'm sick of everything in my wardrobe. Living with Marie-Camille has made me feel like some tramp off the street.'

'Rubbish, you always look great. I've been thinking about what you said and I am not going to let my stupid insecurities spoil my day. I'm excited about Marie-Camille taking us to where the smart shops are. Agathe is looking forward to the day too. She says she hasn't got any spending money for clothes but she says she's happy just to look.'

'I gather Rani has written up a timetable for the day.'

'Of course. If she can't be a vet we all know she's going to be Prime Minister.'

10.00 p.m.

We are back. I am weak with exhaustion. My legs don't work any more.

So much to say, I don't know where to begin so I'll begin with item number one on Rani's Day Out in London list.

Hold on, need a tuna and mayonnaise sandwich. I'm mad about them at the moment. It's all in the lemon and pepper added to the mayo.

10.15 p.m.

Right, I'm ready now.

London Day Out:
8.30 a.m.

Got on train.

Successfully accomplished that – though it was a near thing. Marie-Camille broke her time-in-bathroom record, which meant Mum, who can be a bit anxious about punctuality, was hyper-ventilating all the way to the station. The others were already there. Cécile was looking incredibly cool in slim suede skirt, beautiful leather boots and yet another cashmere top – sleeveless this time. I don't care what anyone says though; Chloe still looked more interesting in her funky customised tweed jacket. Agathe hovered at their side in a mercifully plain skirt and sweatshirt looking excited and happy. Chloe had told me that her parents aren't divorced. Her dad died two years ago and things have been tough for her family since. Chloe really wanted her to have a good day out.

8.40 a.m.

Rani ate her first packed lunch. She always brings two. One for as soon as we get going and one for lunch.

Train really full. Mum and Mrs Ray got seats at other end of carriage. I had to go to the loo (excitement) and by the time I got back to where the others were sitting Rani and Chloe were pointing gleefully to the two seats behind them. I soon saw why: the only free seat left was next to a tall, blond boy of about sixteen. I *hate* sitting next to strangers and boys are the worst. He looked as embarrassed as me and so we both stared fixedly in opposite directions. I could see the back of Chloe and Rani's heads close together muttering to each other in front of us. Suddenly they sank down and disappeared. A few minutes later, after some furtive rustling, two faces slowly rose above the seats. Beaming. They had each pulled all their hair over to one side and put it in a huge sticky out bunch over one ear.

'What do you think? Hey, Carrie. Carrie, yoo-hoo. What do you think of our new hairstyles?' Chloe asked. She patted her curly bunch playfully. 'Pretty cool, hey?'

'Go away,' I hissed.

'What, what was that she said?' Rani asked Chloe. 'He's very,

very good-looking? Is that what you said, Carrie? He's very, very good-looking?'

The boy went scarlet.

'GO AWAY.'

'OK, OK . . . there's no need to be rude. If you don't appreciate our new look . . . Honestly . . .' She raised her eyes at the boy. 'She's supposed to be our friend.' The two faces sank behind the seats again.

I gave the boy an embarrassed half-smile.

'Sorry about that. They're a bit mad. They'll leave me alone now.'

But I spoke too soon.

'Chocka, chocka, chocka, chocka.'

Alarmed, we both looked up.

'CHOCKA, CHOCKA, CHOCKA.' The sound got louder and rising above the top of the seats appeared the whirling hair of Rani and Chloe.

This time they had pulled their hair up and tied it tightly in a band right on top of their heads. Then they had flattened it out so that when they spun their heads around and around it went into a big flat wheel.

'We call this the helicopter look,' Rani puffed, obviously getting a bit dizzy. 'Wotcha think?'

'GO AWAY,' I said again.

Rani stopped twirling her head and rested her chin on the top of the seat. She grinned cheerfully at the boy who gave her a sheepish smile in return.

'She's got a boyfriend, you know.' She nodded in my direction. 'But I'm sure —'

Then she spotted her mum pounding up the carriage and they

shot back in their seats with the speed of light. Maddy and Agathe got the giggles. Mrs Ray's keen eyes did a quick sweep but saw nothing. Rani and Chloe chuckled.

Not sure quite how sophisticated girls about town behave, but I suspect not like that.

9.47 a.m.

Got off at Euston station.

Uneventful, but heavens that boy could run fast. He could be in the Olympic team with the speed he legged it down that platform. I think it was Rani and Chloe offering to do his hair that did it.

10.30 a.m.

Covent Garden.

Wow! Lots of street theatre people. Mostly pretending to be puppets or statues. They stay absolutely still for ages. There was one guy dressed as a Samurai and I swear he never even blinked and Rani was practically up his nose for ages checking for movement. Maddy took loads of photos. Rani, Chloe and I stood very still in tasteful poses hoping for a bit of cash from passers-by. All I can say is that standing absolutely motionless is a lot harder than it looks and some people can be really rude. Marie-Camille whined the whole time about walking on the cobbles. I wonder if heels that high really were the sensible choice for a day of sightseeing and shopping?

12.30 p.m.

Ate packed lunch. Tuna and mayonnaise sandwich. Naturally. Ate it in Trafalgar Square. Gathered strength for the afternoon ahead. Cécile and Marie-Camille sat with their heads together discussing smart shops in French.

2.00 p.m.

Oxford Street.

Huzzah! Mum and Mrs Ray were letting us go off on our own. They left us with strict instructions to stick together and made us check our watches and mobiles in case of being kidnapped or forced into lap dancing and the like. They would meet us back at the Tube stop at 4.45 p.m.

Free at last. And that's when the trouble began.

2.15 p.m.

TopShop.

We got there unmolested. We were excited. We had been looking forward to this for ages and ages.

'TopShop!' snorted Marie-Camille in her French snorting way at the top of the escalator that plunges down into retail heaven. 'Let's go to Bond Street, to the boutiques . . . I want to visit a new one zat has —'

'Come on, Marie-Camille. You *knew* we wanted to go to this shop.'

'But why? If we go to Bond Street, I show you beautiful clothes-ses. Why do you not want to go zere straight away? Why do you want to go 'ere?'

'We can't afford to *buy* anything there, Marie-Camille. We said we would show you the shops we liked and then you could take us to the shops that you go to,' I said, exasperated at how her

'But what about Chloe?' I protested. 'Why can't she come in, you know how much she wants to see those dresses.'

Marie-Camille gave a little sigh and looked Chloe up and down. I got the feeling she'd been waiting for a moment like this ever since she first met her. 'You see, Chloe,' she said. 'You always look very, er . . . *charmante*. You are veree clever with ze old clothes-ses and ze garments not expensive. But . . .' and she shook her sleek little head, 'you maybe do not understand zis place so well, I zink zis will be too . . . maybe, well.' She obviously thought she was about to be tactful here. 'Too *complicated* for you. You live in veree small place. Cécile and me, we are used to zeese places and zeese zings.'

'But you know they've got Lucy Kell designs in there,' Chloe sighed looking at the names etched on the glass. 'And I really would love to see them.'

A shop assistant came up to the window and looked curiously at us. That was enough for Marie-Camille; she took a step into the shop and shut the door firmly in our faces.

'Well really! How rude,' Rani snapped.

'Let's just go in,' I said peering at Marie-Camille and Cécile inside.

'I know, we should all just walk right inside,' Rani pulled herself up to her not-very-full height.

Agathe looked unhappy. 'But we 'ave no money to buy the dress in zis shop. Maybe we should wait here.'

'We can look can't we? It's not illegal.' Rani had stuck her tongue out at Marie-Camille and it had not gone down well. Cécile appeared to be very busy looking at dresses and to have forgotten we were there. We all looked at each other, embarrassed at being intimidated by something as silly as going into a shop.

'What's up, everyone?' It was Maddy, back from the camera shop. She glanced up at the shop. 'What are you all doing standing outside on the street?'

'Marie-Camille and Cécile are inside, and Marie-Camille didn't seem to think that we would, er . . . quite fit in there,' I answered.

Maddy looked up and scanned the name of the shop. 'But Chloe, this place is where Lucy Kell sells her designs.'

'*I know*,' Chloe said, agonised, 'but firstly Marie-Camille said we couldn't go in because we're not wearing smart enough clothes, and then she said I didn't know anything about real fashion anyway, and now I feel too weird to go in.'

Maddy looked at our sheepish faces with a bemused expression.

'Jeez, what are you guys *like*?' She grinned. 'Follow me.' She pushed the door open.

The rest of us trooped meekly after her. All except the timid Agathe, who said she'd just wait outside and see what happened. Marie-Camille, who had been talking to an elegant sales assistant, turned in horror at our entrance, then coolly turned her back to us. Cécile, who had been looking along a rack, scooted up a spiral staircase to the upper floor of the shop.

'Coo-eee!' said Rani, waving. Marie-Camille's face was thunder. She began to speak rapidly in French to the assistant whose smiling expression swiftly changed and she trotted quickly up the stairs.

We gathered round her.

'What did you say to her?' I asked nervously. 'Because, call me psychic, but it wasn't anything good, was it?'

Marie-Camille's eyes widened innocently. 'I zay nuzzing. I zink she just see zat you are not the usual people 'ere and she worry. She goes to find the manageress. I zink it better zat you leave before she come.'

'But why?' Rani said, frowning.

'*Faites attention. Ces anglaises ne savent pas se conduire.* Isn't that what you said?' Maddy asked, looking coolly at Marie-Camille. 'I am going to tell the manageress when she re-appears that we *do* know how to behave and it's quite safe for her to let us look around, even though, as you just said, we're not the sort of people who are used to being in places like this. I think we'll somehow control our shop-lifting and vandalism tendencies.'

Marie-Camille's jaw dropped.

'*Mais tu parles* . . . you speak . . .'

'*Oui, je parle français.*' Maddy interrupted. 'Which is just as well in the circumstances, isn't it?'

Before we had time to take everything in, Marie-Camille had recovered enough to lean forward and whisper, 'The manageress knows my mother veree well; we spend much money in this shop in Paris. And you?' She waved her hand at us. 'The manageress she will not believe you.' She looked Maddy up and down. ''Ave you ever been in a place like zis before? Don't you just feel a little uncomfortable, a little, how do you say . . . out of the depth?'

'No,' Maddy said calmly. 'I don't.'

The manageress was clattering down the staircase closely followed by the sales assistant and then Cécile. Marie-Camille stepped coyly to one side and looked up at her. The woman stopped halfway down and stared at us. Suddenly her face broke into a warm smile and she outstretched her arms.

'Maddy Van de Velde!'

Maddy beamed in return. 'Madame Blanche!'

To the astonishment of everyone Madame Blanche ran down the last few stairs and planted two big kisses on Maddy's cheeks. And then off they went into a French gabble, the subject of which obviously caused Marie-Camille a great deal of pain. Eventually the manageress turned to Marie-Camille. 'But these are your friends,' she said puzzled. 'I think there has been some mistake, has there not?'

Marie-Camille could do nothing but give a sheepish nod.

Maddy then introduced us. I have to say I did still feel quite shy. She said something else to the sales assistant who nodded and looked kindly at Chloe.

'The Lucy Kell clothes are upstairs. She's going to show them to you,' Maddy said, smiling.

Chloe disappeared in a daze after the assistant.

Marie-Camille found her voice again. 'You, you *know* Madame Blanche?'

'Yes, when we lived in Paris I would often go to the Paris shop with my mother, or my dad, I just didn't know that they had opened a London shop.'

'Yes,' Madame Blanche explained. 'I have been here for a year now, to train the assistants to the highest standard. Maddy, it is so good to see you. How is your father, the wonderful Daniel Van de Velde? Now he is a man who understands fashion . . .'

Marie-Camille's and Cécile's jaws dropped.

'Your father . . . your father, 'e is Daniel Van de Velde? I never . . . I not know zis . . .' Marie-Camille spluttered.

Maddy turned slowly towards her then flashed her a dazzling smile.

'I *know*.' She waggled her hands in the air. 'SURPRISE! And do you know something else. He's going to judge the competition!'

Further jaw dropping.

'And your mother, Marie-Camille?' Madame Blanche asked politely.

Marie-Camille rallied, obviously pleased to be back on safe ground after the trauma of the last few minutes. Of course her mother was well, she gushed, but very busy, what more would you expect from a top Parisian socialite?

'Absolutely.' Madame Blanche nodded. 'And it was so lovely to see her here two days ago. But she didn't mention that we would be having the pleasure of seeing you too! She was having just the little visit on her way to . . . where? Now I cannot remember. You will have to help me here, Marie-Camille . . .'

Marie-Camille flushed a deep red. We all tried to look as if we hadn't heard but of course she knew we had.

'My mother is so busy, Madame Blanche, it is very difficult to keep track of all her travels. Of course I knew she was coming to London. But I could not see her. I am with my school programme you see.'

It was so obvious she hadn't known. She would have gone on about it for ever if she had. I wondered if her mother actually knew where her daughter was? The housekeeper and driver seemed to be the only ones who really knew what was going on in her life and even then they didn't know the half of it.

Madame Blanche opened her mouth to say something but then looked at Marie-Camille's face and thought better of it. Instead she lied graciously. 'Of course, of course, I think now I remember . . . now, let me show you what we have here.'

She gave us a guided tour of all the clothes and let us try some on.

Looking in the mirror, wearing a long velvet dress, I truly felt like a princess. At least I could say that I once wore a dress worth £1,545 (I asked – they didn't have price tags).

Though we got Agathe in through the door, no one could persuade her to try anything on. TopShop had been enough style excitement for her in one day. Eventually Chloe came back down the stairs looking flushed. The assistant said something in French to Madame Blanche and the manageress smiled at Marie-Camille and Cécile waiting at the door.

'Your friend has a true understanding of fashion. A real intelligent understanding. A gift. I am sure she will be well known to us all one day.'

I looked at Chloe and saw how much it meant to her. I knew that this was a very special moment in her life. I was glad I was there to see it.

The same could not be said of Marie-Camille. Who did not look very glad at all.

4.40 p.m.
Ran to Tube.

5.20 p.m.
Collapsed on the train. Tuna and mayonnaise sandwich. Tea. Crisps. Muffin. Exhausted.

11.20 p.m.
Still am. Too tired to write anything else. Must sleep.

 CARRIE'S TIP • • • • • • • • • • • • • • • • • •

Make a memories area in your room. Use postcards from
places you've visited or from friends; photos; train and
concert tickets – anything that brings back a good memory
and stick it on. You can use the front or side of your
wardrobe, cover a screen or just stick them around a
corner of your room. (Check with someone to see what you
should use to stick things – people can be quite snappy
about this. How was I supposed to know that superglue was
that strong?)

Chapter 15

Sunday 9.00 a.m.

Marie-Camille in *très, très* bad mood.

I have brought my tea and toast up here. To escape. I cannot be in a bad mood because Jack and Tom are back from Wales. We are meeting them in The Coffee Bean later. I don't want anything to spoil the day. I want my aura to be calm. I can still hear her ranting to Ned and Dad (even Ned's glazed over now), about how downhill the London shops had gone and how they knew nothing about style and she couldn't understand why her mum still went in there. She could barely look at Chloe on the journey home. As if it was somehow all her fault. Yet again I got the last seat, miles away from them but this time it was next to Mum and I told her about our day. When we got back Mum took Marie-Camille up toasted cheese and a bowl of tomato soup and stayed talking to her in her room for a while. None for me. Dr Jennings take note: double standards in my house. Virtue is not always rewarded.

I feel it is beyond hope that Marie-Camille and I could ever be friends. My spooky psychic powers have tragically failed me.

Mum came and knocked on my door with a cup of tea. It's something I suppose.

'Don't be too hard on her,' she pleaded. 'It was tough for her to hear her mum had paid a fleeting visit to London and not told her.'

'I don't know, Mum. It's not like her mum doesn't care about her. There's nothing she can't have.'

'And that's important is it? Having things? You think her life is wonderful, don't you?'

Duh! 'I don't think it, Mum. I can see it for myself. If I had what she had, I'd be nice all the time . . .'

'Wouldn't you rather have my time and attention than a pile of designer clothes, make-up and accessories?' Mum wasn't helping herself here. Then she saw my expression and went on. 'Living in a great big flat on your own most of the time with just staff for company?'

See what I mean? Not helping herself at all. I couldn't help grinning. 'Are you *kidding* me, Mum?'

She laughed and said she knew I understood what she was talking about.

Thought about Rani. I think she would love a bit of hands-off parenting. Cécile's parents are coming over to London this week for some International Lawyers' Conference. They are going to take the opportunity to come up to Boughton and watch the competition on Friday. Rani is beside herself.

She reckons she can only hold off getting her *I'm totally MENTAL about MATHS* badge for so long. It's not that Rani doesn't like maths. She does. It's just that she works so hard in all subjects already. I don't think you could cram any more knowledge into her.

Noooo. Marie-Camille has just come upstairs and beat me into the bathroom. And I've only got four hours to get ready. My spot has gone though.

9.30 a.m.
Rani rang.

'How is the Paris Pain this morning? Is she OK?'

'She's like an angry wasp. I think someone's going to get stung before the end of the day. How's Cécile?'

'She just can't get over the fact Maddy's dad is Daniel Van de Velde. It's been questions, questions since we got back. I think she feels she's missed an opportunity there. She's taking her mind off it by getting very glammed up for this afternoon. She's making a big effort.'

'Oh God. I am actually feeling a chill around my heart.'

'Why?'

'Don't you see? They're going to steal our menfolk, run off with them, leaving us lonely and abandoned.'

'In the time it takes to polish off one hot chocolate and a doughnut?'

'Yes! They don't need long. They move fast, these Continental types . . .'

'Get a grip, Carrie. I can hardly see Marie-Camille causing too much damage in a couple of hours.'

'That's with what you know,' I muttered darkly. 'You haven't seen the mood she's in this morning.'

Rani laughed and said she'd see me later. But I know my psychology. I had worked out that if you add together:

1) The Wayne Brennan disaster (for which I was still held personally responsible), and

2) The events of the London trip yesterday,

you get people who don't think they owe you any favours. And people who are not kindly disposed towards you tend not to care too much about messing with your love life.

That's all I'm saying.

12.00 a.m.

I am dressed at last. I am in my TopShop dress and shoes. One big problem: it is too warm for my camouflage black tights today and my pale legs are sticking out of my TopShop dress like two long, uncooked baguettes.

Marie-Camille has just emerged from her room. Ready to go out. Stunning in tiny white T-shirt, *no bra*, white cotton mini and silver sandals. Marvellous. Why do French girls *always* have tanned legs? And no freckles on their knees? Took one look at Marie-Camille, managed feeble smile, walked straight back in my room, phoned Rani.

'*Iyamdooooomed.*'

'OK, Carrie. Calm down. I'll say this only once. Jack thinks you are wonderful. He adores you. You have nothing to worry about. *And your legs are great.* We are going to have a *wonderful* day. So *stop* worrying.'

10.00 p.m.

Which showed how much she knew.

Mum gave us a lift into town after making Marie-Camille go upstairs and put a bra on which was sooo embarrassing but I couldn't deny being relieved. We picked up Cécile and Rani on the way. Cécile was in a little grey sleeveless shift dress with a frill at the bottom. That sounds boring when I write it down, but it fitted her like a dream. With her delicate black strappy sandals and black patent leather bag, she looked every inch the Parisian girl about town.

I couldn't have been more thrilled.

Jack was waiting outside, looking tanned and fit. As I walked towards him I was thinking, *I will not run. I will not run.* But when he saw me he started to move towards me and I have to admit to breaking into a kind of skippy-trot. But I think I got away with it and it didn't matter anyway – I could tell he was really very, very happy to see me. When he let me go and I got my breath back I thought what a fool I was to worry about anything at all. Jack was back. He had missed me. All was well with the world.

Rani had tactfully swept Marie-Camille and Cécile inside. Tom and Chloe appeared beside us on the pavement. Tom had wanted to put some credit on his mobile at the newsagent's. He was planning to make up for lost time.

'Hi, Carrie,' Tom said, beaming. 'How's it going? Chloe says you've all been having quite a time. I want all the details.' He looked around. 'Where are they then?'

'They've just gone inside with Rani.'

'Well, if they're anything as delightful as Agathe,' Tom went on, 'who for some crazy reason feels she needs to put in an afternoon on some English project, I can't wait to see them. Come on, what are we waiting for?'

'Wait!'

Yes – that was my voice.

'I just want to say one thing to Jack before we go in.'

Everyone looked at me expectantly. I took a deep breath.

'Well, it's this. You know Marie-Camille and I have not necessarily had an easy relationship.'

'I don't think anyone's had an easy relationship with her to be honest,' Chloe added.

'And, erm . . .'

God. Why oh why had I started this? Could I be the uncoolest person in the whole wide world? I think this was about to be the new number one in my dog-person acts of foolishness. A dog-person wants everyone to love them, tries too hard and says too much. What had happened to Carrie, cool, self-assured cat-person? But could I stop myself? Nooo.

'I think she might be a bit flirty with you, Jack.'

Jack's eyes crinkled like he might be suppressing a laugh. He leaned forward as if he was slightly deaf.

'What was that, Carrie? A bit *what*?'

He wasn't going to make this easy.

'A bit flirty,' I mumbled. I could see Chloe behind him, shaking her head sadly at me.

'And why would that be? Apart from my obvious good looks, charm, intelligence, etc.'

I ticked the reasons off on my fingers.

'Well, one, I sort of told her Wayne Brennan was a famous rock star and two, she's really annoyed about the manageress of the shop telling Chloe she was so talented when she'd been so snooty about us even going in there. Three, there was the whole thing about Maddy being able to speak French and her dad being Daniel Van de Velde and me not telling her about *him* . . .'

Jack nodded sagely. 'Well, that all makes perfect sense.'

'I'll explain in more detail later.'

'I'll look forward to it. But hey! Thanks for the warning. Whatever might have happened? I can't bear to think. I haven't even met her and already I feel so . . .' He bit his knuckle. '. . . so *used*.'

'Well, this I've got to see,' Tom said, pushing us all inside.

We joined Marie-Camille, Cécile and Rani in the queue. I took another deep breath.

'Jack, this is Marie-Camille and Cécile.'

The French girls both gave him a friendly hello but to my surprise Marie-Camille didn't make a huge fuss or anything. Cunning, I thought. She was obviously going to be more subtle about this than I had given her credit for. Cat-person, you see. Chloe gave me a what-were-you-worrying-about look. Tom had disappeared to grab a table.

'What on earth are *they* doing here?' Rani hissed at me and rolled her eyes in the direction of the back of the room.

At the back of the café, Manon and Océane were happily ensconced in a booth with Kenny and Joe Carter. I had a suspicion that Joe rather liked Maddy but she had unexpectedly cried off coming out with us today. She said she needed to catch up on developing her photos at home.

Marie-Camille smiled serenely behind us. 'Oh, do I not say? I tell zem we come today. I say it OK if zey come too.'

Rani gave her a tight smile and went over to say hello to Kenny who was now waving frantically at her.

'You must be ze Tom.' Marie-Camille immediately squeezed herself in the small space next to him on the end of the bench. With his broad stocky frame and thick shock of dark hair, Tom took up a lot of room. She barely acknowledged Chloe. Jack and I sat with Cécile on the other side of the table.

Something very strange was going on. I suddenly realised what it was: Marie-Camille was not gazing at Jack with mega-watt interest on her face; she was gazing up at *Tom*.

Because it was Tom, he hadn't worked it out yet and he was looking expectantly at Jack and grinning. He then turned to Marie-Camille to see what she was up to and found himself staring straight into the intense beam of her brown eyes. He reared back.

'Whaoh! Hello there. Mmm . . . Marie-Camille.'

'Hello there, Tom,' she purred.

Tom turned swiftly to raise a thick eyebrow at Chloe. She grinned and he swivelled round again to Marie-Camille. 'Er . . . how have you enjoyed your stay so far?'

She sighed. 'It's wonderful. I see many much of your lovely country. I had wonderful visit to London. And in school I make beautiful dress you know. For ze fashion show. Cécile also.'

'That's right,' Tom nodded. 'Chloe told me you had all been designing dresses. Chloe is amazing at stuff like that.'

'Mmm . . . such a pity for her that her design is not chosen for the competition. That her group prefer the dress of Cécile. Is that not so, Chloe?'

'Cécile's dress was a wonderful design,' Chloe responded. Which was a gracious response. My response was an overwhelming desire to lean over and rub my chocolate cake all over Marie-Camille's shiny, clean hair.

'Really? Well, I'm sure it is . . .' Tom looked confused. I have noticed boys always tend to be a couple of laps behind when it comes to catching on to this sort of nastiness.

'Hem, hem.' I coughed. 'I think Cécile's dress is such a success because it has been a real team effort with everyone pulling their weight. You know, no one person dictating to the others, forcing them to do only what *they* want.'

Marie-Camille gave a tinkling laugh, narrowed her eyes at me, and turned back to Tom.

'You must find life here is very different to Paris I suppose.' He ploughed on cheerily.

'Oh, so different. Here very quiet, but great people. I just *love* English people . . .'

Chloe was trying desperately to look like she was taking this mega-flirt seriously and struggling to pull her features into an annoyed expression. She was failing.

Tom was now fully appreciative of the situation and determined to enjoy every minute. 'And why is that?' He continued coyly. Was he actually batting his lashes?

'Why?' She gave him a cheeky look. 'Because zey are so charming, so polite, so gentlemen . . .'

Gentlemen! Excuse me. That's not what she was saying after a night on the tiles with Wayne Brennan. But she wasn't finished yet.

'I zink girls in France always zink ze English boys are so more interesting.' She was practically leaning on his shoulder and looking up at him like he was the most fascinating person in the world. Chloe rolled her eyes at me. I felt Jack's knee press against mine.

'Tell me more,' Tom went on, warming to this theme and returning her cheeky grin.

'Now you are teasing me!' She slapped at his sleeve. 'Wanting more of the compliments from ze French girl. I say no more on this subject. You will get, how do you say? Ze big head!'

Chloe and I snorted.

But then Chris Jones came in the door. And if you didn't know what a prat he was you would have to say that he was looking gorgeous. He must have been studying on a sun lounger because his long hair had got bleached even blonder and his green-blue eyes seemed an even deeper colour in his tanned face. Marie-Camille must have seen Jack and me look up because she turned round and saw him. Tom meanwhile was oblivious to his arrival.

'You must tell me more. Do go on. Why *are* English guys superior in every way?'

But he had lost his audience. Poor guy, he didn't stand a chance. Chris began to make his way over.

'Who is zat?' she asked casually. (As if we'd be fooled.)

I leaned forward. 'That's Chris Jones.' And then I said, out of badness, 'He's the lead singer in a band.'

She shot me a suspicious glance.

'No really, he is. He's the lead singer in a band with Jack.'

Jack nodded. 'He is, I promise. NOT a famous band though . . .' He caught my eye.

This didn't seem to matter to Marie-Camille this time round.

'I think I should tell you something; Chris has a . . .'

But before I could say anything more Chris had slid alongside our table and was giving me the benefit of his full-beam smile.

'Hi, Carrie. How's it going?'

As I'd hardly spoken to him since the him-snogging-Jet incident I was surprised to be spoken to as if I was one of his best friends. Mind you, I hadn't seen him without Jennifer before now.

'Fine,' I said flatly. I still think he's a jerk.

He flushed under his tan, paused then leaned forward. 'Now who is this?' he cooed at Marie-Camille. 'One of our lovely French visitors I would guess?'

Marie-Camille giggled at him from under her perfectly curled eyelashes.

'But there's hardly any room for you here! Won't you and your friend come and join me on another table so I don't have to be all on my own?'

Marie-Camille and Cécile looked at each other. Cécile looked reluctant but Marie-Camille gave her a pleading look and after a brief jabber in French, where Cécile sounded pretty cross, they both got up from the table. Some things are the same in any language.

'Hey, Jack, need to talk to you about some band stuff before you go,' said Chris, doing his pointy-click thing.

'Gotcha.' Jack pointy-clicked back.

Just as well Chris Jones doesn't get sarcasm.

'Er, what just happened?' Tom protested. 'It was all going so brilliantly, I was well in there . . .'

'Come on, mate,' Jack said. 'Chloe has simply appeared to have upset Marie-Camille even more than Carrie – which has to be quite an achievement. That's why she was all over you.'

'*I KNOW that's why.* But I was still enjoying myself.'

'Have you no pride, Tom?' Chloe laughed.

'No! Fit French bird chatting me up? Absolutely not. I'm grateful for whatever crumbs are thrown my way.'

'Even if it was a hideous sight to behold for the rest of us,' I added.

'Jealousy, jealousy.' Tom sighed. 'Was it very painful for you to watch, my darling?' he cooed at Chloe.

'It was,' Chloe said firmly. 'I thought that at any second she was going to squeeze your manly biceps and tell you "how beeg and strrrong you are".'

Tom looked wistful. 'Well, I'm disappointed. I didn't get to flirt back properly at all, and I was thinking of some great lines and everything. And I got nowhere near the bit where I had to say, "Back off, babe. Keep your French mitts to yourself".'

'I should hope not! She knew you were going out with me!' Chloe protested. 'I just call that really bad manners.'

'What's bad manners?' Rani had come over to join us.

'Trying to get off with someone else's boyfriend. When they are sitting right next to you.'

'Oh, right.'

She looked over at Manon and Océane giggling away with Kenny and Joe. She wasn't happy but I knew she wouldn't want to discuss it in front of Tom and Jack.

'Well, if you're on that subject,' she went on, 'isn't Chris living a bit dangerously chatting up Marie-Camille like that when Jennifer might come in at any moment?'

'No danger,' Rani volunteered. 'Cara told me Jennifer had to go away with her parents and Katia for the weekend to visit relatives. Apparently it required a straightjacket, chains and lashing her kicking and screaming to the roof-rack, but they dragged her away from her beloved in the end. Not that she's seen that much of him. She's not back till this evening.'

'She won't be too pleased if she hears about this,' Tom sniffed. 'Marie-Camille's very free with her affections, isn't she? Behaviour like that can hurt the more sensitive person, you know.'

'Don't worry about Chris,' Jack replied coolly. 'We all know what a smooth operator *he* is.'

I pulled a face at him. Sometimes I wonder if Jack *is* the tiniest bit jealous of my fling-ette with Chris.

Tom tapped his watch. 'Come on, guys, we're going to miss the film. Is Kenny coming, Rani, or have we lost some of our party this afternoon?'

Rani stuck her nose in the air. 'Kenny can do what he likes;

he's a free agent. But we do need to tell Marie-Camille and Cécile we have to go.'

'OK,' Tom said as he held up his hands, 'only asking.'

Jack remembered he had to talk to Chris. He said he'd tell the girls we were going and meet us outside.

'I'll be two seconds.'

Ten minutes later we were still waiting on the pavement.

Suddenly Océane, Manon, Kenny and Joe all burst out together.

'We come wiz you to see film,' the girls chorused.

Rani looked particularly delighted.

Jack wandered out of the café at last. With Cécile only. He put his arm across my shoulder. 'Marie-Camille says can we pick her up after the film. She's going to hang out here for a while with Chris. Sorry I was so long; Cécile was talking to Chris and me about the instruments she plays. Amazing! She's going to come and jam a bit with the band on the keyboards tomorrow at the rehearsal.'

'Excellent!' Tom exclaimed. 'Can we all come?'

Cécile made noises about being embarrassed to play in front of so many people.

'Don't be so modest, Cécile.' Jack laughed. 'I can tell you probably play better than any of us. And that's in ten minutes of knowing you. It'll be fun.' Cécile gave him a grateful smile. As Jack turned to talk to Tom she saw me watching her. She smiled again.

What had Rani said earlier? 'Stop worrying.'

I don't think so. I think my worries have just begun.

Vintage jeans and low-waisted skirts that are just slightly too big can be slimming. Jackets on the other hand should fit well or else they can swamp you or look boxy. As a rule baggy clothes are rarely flattering as an all over look. Team them with other things — like loose trousers with a skinny T-shirt, or a big sweater with slim-fit jeans.

Chapter 16

Monday 7.25 a.m.

Woke with sense of unease. Dr Jennings, please take note: sometimes youth is not all it's cracked up to be.

By the end of yesterday it was obvious that Jack thought that:

a) Marie-Camille was fun but tricky;
b) Manon and Océane had the intelligence of pond life;
c) Cécile was the most talented and cool girl in the whole world.

Rani could have been more sympathetic.

'Now you know what it's been like living with her all this time. It's been hell. Has anyone listened? Nooo. I just can't compete. She *is* Miss Perfect. And it's the quiet way she gets everyone in my family to do what she wants . . .'

'But I don't want Jack to do what she wants! Now you've put a horrible image in my head.'

'Relax. Jack loves music. He's impressed by all the instruments she plays, that's all.'

'I just don't want her playing with his instrument, that's all.'

'Carrie! I'm shocked. You're obviously deranged with paranoia. She's not going to be playing anyone's instrument. And actually, I'll let you in on an interesting fact about Cécile and her music . . .'

'What is it?'

'She's not that brilliant.'

'Seriously?'

'Seriously. Oh, she plays everything well. She practises all the time and has obviously been doing so for years and years. But she's not actually that *naturally* talented.'

I paused.

'Look, no offence, Rani, but how would you know?'

Neither Rani nor myself could count ourselves as musical, as Mrs Cotton our long-suffering piano teacher through Years Three and Four could verify.

'None taken. My mum told me.'

'Well, that's a bit weird, isn't it? I thought her sister was a musical genius.'

'She is. But according to my mum, Cécile isn't.'

I found this immensely cheering. But I was forgetting another of Rani's problems.

'How's Kenny?'

'Fine.'

'Come on; don't give me "fine". What's going on?'

'Nothing. It's not like he's really my boyfriend or anything. He and Joe seemed to have the *best* time with Manon and Océane. Frankly, I'm disappointed in their poor taste. I don't know how Sasha and Melanie put up with them. No wonder they wanted to go shopping together and leave them to us.'

'Have you spoken to him about it?'

'To say what? I don't want to get more serious with you but I don't want you to be best friends with any other girls? Sounds a bit pathetic.

'He's *not* going to be best friends with them. They *are* going home on Saturday you know.'

'A lot can happen in a few days,' she replied darkly.

'*For God's sake, don't say that!*' I wailed.

9.00 p.m.

Let's start with the good news. Yes, let's get that out of the way before the VERY VERY BAD NEWS.

First thing in the art room, Mrs Crowe told us that Tess, Gemma and both their exchanges had all gone down with the bug. It looks like they won't be back in school till the end of the week. (This is not the good news, by the way.)

'There's space now in the competition for another dress,' Rani hissed at me as she tried to avoid treading on the skirt Jennifer's team was working on. Difficult – there was about nine million yards of it. 'I'm going to see if I can get Chloe a chance to make hers.' She put her finger to her lips. 'Say nothing, OK? I don't want to get her hopes up.'

I grabbed her sleeve. 'What about Gemma and Tess?' I hated to put a damper on her idea, but I knew Mrs Crowe.

'Shhhh! They've hardly got anywhere in their team. Tess and Gemma have never agreed which design to go for. First they argued, now they won't speak to one another. The French girls have been stuck in the middle of it. No one's got anywhere with the sewing . . .'

'Er, don't you think you should ask Chloe first? And what will Cécile and Marie-Camille say?'

I cast a look on the other side of the room where Marie-Camille was picking out beads for the neckline.

Last night I had decided to let her know about Chris and Jennifer.

'I know zis already,' she sighed. 'She shout about 'im all ze time on ze bus, but I know 'e like me better.'

'He really isn't a very nice guy at all, Marie-Camille. Please take my advice. Have nothing to do with him. He is *bad* news.'

She gave me a sly smile.

'I think you like 'im for yourself? *Non*? 'E was your boyfriend. Now you 'ave Jack. Maybe you like Chris more?'

'God, no! And he was never really my boyfriend. I could not be less interested.'

'I zink 'e is very handsome, *n'est-ce pas*? It is sad he not come to school every day now. At least he come for zis rehearsal.' She sighed.

I gave up. At least I'd tried.

I noticed that she was steering well clear of Jennifer in the art room this morning. Jennifer was a girl of extreme passions and word had obviously not reached her about Chris's flirtation. I am also a girl of extreme passions but I gave Cécile a normal greeting on the bus. Sometimes, when they really need to, dog-people can pull cool out of the bag too. And maybe I was making a fuss about nothing anyway. Although I said that Cécile had impressed him, to be fair, Jack *had* been lovely to me for the rest of the day.

'You know how jealous of Chloe Marie-Camille is,' I warned Rani. 'She was jealous of her before London; after Madame Blanche's praise she's never going to give her a break. She feels Chloe humiliated her somehow in that shop. She would still be trying to climb on to Tom's lap now if Chris Jones hadn't come in and distracted her. She won't be willing to agree. And there's so little time as well.'

'It's not really up to Marie-Camille, it's more up to Cécile as

Chloe's on her team. And we've nearly finished her dress. I think she'll be OK. Even if they do make a fuss, they can't really complain because we'll do it after school. I've been thinking about it and if we meet up every night after school and in breaks and things we will be able to get it done. I know we will. She cannot miss this chance to let Maddy's dad see one of her designs.' Rani's eyes shone with excitement.

'Oh well, my fingers are pincushions already. A few more holes won't hurt. Let's go for it.' I waggled them for effect.

'It's going to be great.' She beamed. 'I know we can do it. I just know it.'

I went down to lunch, and Maddy was first down after me. I told her the good news.

'So wouldn't that be great, if Mrs Crowe agreed? You loved Chloe's design.'

'Yeah, sure I did.' She didn't sound very enthusiastic. In fact she seemed positively low. And she'd not said a word on the bus either. In spite of Marie-Camille and Cécile desperately trying to be friendly. I wonder why?

'Photography going OK?' I asked.

'Mmm? Yeah, good, really good. I've got some great pictures. It's been a really interesting project.'

'So?'

'So?'

'So why do you look like a wet weekend? What's up?'

Maddy sighed and pushed her chicken salad around her plate. She cast her eyes quickly around her before speaking. 'Look, everyone will know soon enough. But it's not going to be offi-cially announced till a meeting after school today.'

'What?'

She sighed. 'My dad won't be able to judge the competition. He has to be in New York. There's nothing he can do about it apparently. It's a last minute crisis. He told me yesterday. It's why I didn't come out with you. I felt so awful.'

The implications of what she had just said sank in. 'Oh my God, what's going to happen? Marie-Camille told all the exchanges and now *everyone* knows and is really excited.'

Maddy put her head in her hands. 'I know, I know. But I can't do anything about it. He phoned Mrs Crowe this morning. You absolutely must swear not to tell anyone about it. Not even Rani or Chloe. Mrs Crowe doesn't want anyone to know till after school today.'

I swore.

'She hadn't had time to ask someone else to judge. She wanted to be able to tell us who will be taking my dad's place.'

'So, who's it going to be?'

She winced. 'Mrs Crowe said that Mrs McGuy had volunteered.'

'Mrs McGuy!' Surely my ears were deceiving me? 'But she's worn the same tweed skirt for ten thousand years. I'm sure it's welded to her body. It's not that she knows absolutely nothing about fashion AT ALL, it's worse than that; she is anti-fashion, the designer destroyer, the philistine of the frocks . . .'

'Jeez, OK, OK,' Maddy cried. 'I get your point.'

And then I felt dreadful for ranting on and making her feel worse. I gave her a hug.

'Sorry, Maddy, what was I thinking? I'm an insensitive, selfish pig.'

'Oooh, don't you think you're being just a teeny bit hard on yourself?'

It was Rani, back from her visit with Mrs Crowe. Maddy gave me a warning look, but she needn't have worried. Rani was bursting with her news, oblivious to anything else. Mrs Crowe had said yes! Rani said it was like she really didn't mind what anyone did. They had phoned Tess and Gemma on their sickbeds and they were delighted to have a way out of the project. Apparently, they were both relieved that the other one wasn't going to win. The French girls were just delighted not to be in a war zone any more and to be able to get on with being ill in peace.

Then Chloe appeared and Rani patted the seat next to her.

'Sit down, me old shipmate,' she said. 'I've got some news.'

I caught Maddy's eye. She was biting the sleeve of her jumper.

After Rani told her, Chloe went all pink and tried very hard not show how excited she was. I felt so bad. I knew she was going to be desperately disappointed.

When she got up to leave she said, 'Thanks so, so, much. I can't believe Daniel Van de Velde will actually see one of my designs. It's going to be one of the best nights of my life.'

Maddy startled her by leaping up from the table and disappearing into the crowded lunch hall.

'What's up with her?' Rani asked.

I shrugged my shoulders.

I felt life was horribly cruel sometimes. I knew that Chloe, who never does anyone any harm, was going to be so crushed when she heard about Maddy's dad not being able to judge the competition. She'd try not to show it though. Compare her to Marie-Camille who has everything and complains all the time. Chloe has not had it easy: since her parents split up they don't have much money and she has to do loads around the house to help her mum and Jim. She never complains. Why can't she have a break? It's not fair.

When we got to the art room just after last bell, Mrs Crowe wasn't there. There was a notice on the board. We gathered around with the French girls who were back from their afternoon at the Middleton Museum.

'Madame Debas say museum veree interesting,' Katia had told me chirpily this morning. As she returned she muttered to me as she went past. 'Zat Madame Debas. She *lie*.'

The notice said:

I regret to announce that, due to unforeseen circumstances, Daniel Van de Velde will not be able to judge the Black and White Fashion Show. Mrs McGuy has kindly agreed to take his place.
Mrs Crowe

Chloe's face fell.

I put my arm around her. 'Maddy feels so bad about it, Chloe. She knows how much everyone was looking forward to it. Maybe you don't want to make your design now but I still think we should do it. We really, really should. Just to see it on the catwalk.'

'I so agree,' squeaked Rani, still shocked by the news. 'It's a fantastic design and we don't care that he won't be there. We'll help you: we won't rest until we see you modelling it.'

Chloe squared her shoulders and managed a smile. 'Well, OK then. I mean, it's not all about who the judge is. That's not the right spirit. At least Cécile isn't going to complain now.'

Marie-Camille was yakking furiously to Cécile, as expected. I tapped her on the shoulder so she continued in English for our benefit. 'I work and work, and for why do I work? For nuzzing. For this Madame McGuy mountain in her 'orrible rough clothe-ses to judge my design. It is too 'orrible. It is like a bad joke, I zink.'

Cécile was looking pale. Maybe she was going to get the bug too. Fingers crossed. No, I don't mean that.

I began. 'We were wondering, er . . . you know that Tess, Gemma and their exchanges are ill?'

Marie-Camille looked at us as if to say 'So? And this affects me how?'

I nudged Chloe.

'Well, they won't be able to finish their dress.' She bit her lip.

Cécile frowned, slightly irritated by what she obviously regarded as an irrelevant turn in the conversation.

'So there's a space in the competition, and Mrs Crowe has said that we can make up my dress.' Chloe hurried on. 'Don't worry, Cécile, your design will be our priority. It's just that you know we're nearly finished now,' she added. 'We'll make mine after school.'

Cécile looked at Marie-Camille.

Marie-Camille shrugged.

'Zere is no real competition for us, now we 'ave the hairy lady for judging. I zink impossible to finish in time anyway . . . Poor Chloe, you get ze chance to show your dress and now we 'ave no Daniel Van de Velde.' But she didn't sound that sorry for her.

Cécile said nothing. You could see the disappointment of the news and its repercussions had hit her particularly hard. Was she upset because her parents may decide not to come up from

London now? Sometimes it was very difficult to work out what she was thinking. Eventually she said, 'I think Marie-Camille is correct. You 'ave not the time and now Daniel Van de Velde does not come. I cannot see why you want to do zis, all ze work . . . for no real competition.'

'But we do!' Rani cried. 'We really do. We don't care about the competition, we just want to see the dress made up.'

Cécile shrugged her shoulders in resignation. 'OK. It is true my dress is nearly finish.'

'Thank you!' Chloe cried. 'We'll work just as hard on your dress as we always have, I promise. It's just that it's a great opportunity to do my own thing. Normally I just mess about adapting other people's clothes but to do one of my own designs from scratch . . .'

But Marie-Camille and Cécile weren't listening. Mrs Crowe had come back and was clapping her hands, gathering everyone around.

'Listen, listen. The most exciting news. I have just come off the phone from speaking to Daniel Van de Velde again. No, no,' she said, raising her hand. 'I'm afraid he *hasn't* been able to re-arrange his schedule, Marie-Camille.'

General deflated groan.

'No, *he* won't be able to come but he has got *someone else* to come to take his place. A personal friend.'

She had everyone's attention now.

'Girls, *Lucy Kell*, the top British designer will be judging our competition on Friday.'

And pandemonium broke out. Because *that* was the great news.

9.45 p.m.

If only the day had ended there. But it didn't.

I will need a large bar of chocolate to get me through writing the next bit. I'm off to the kitchen. I am hoping to avoid Ned who has inexplicably not yet been fired from the lead in *Joseph*. It's been 'Close Every Door to Me' wafting round this house for ages and the art room now has a life-sized camel and too many palm trees all over the place. They will be performing it this week. We have to go with the French girls on Wednesday night. If he thinks Marie-Camille is going to be impressed by the sight of him in a loincloth, he is very much mistaken.

10.05 p.m.

What a day.

After the meeting, as we walked down the stairs to the music room, I realised I hadn't spotted that Cécile was wearing a small crêpe bandage around one wrist.

'Cécile's sprained her hand,' Rani explained, giving me a meaningful look. 'She won't be able to play to her usual standard . . .'

'Are you going to watch ze rehearsal?' Cécile interrupted. 'Or will you 'ave to make ze dress?'

'We're going to stay for fifteen minutes,' I said firmly. 'Then we're going round to Chloe's. Mum's going to take you and Marie-Camille home later.'

'Zat is a shame for you to miss zis,' she said in a sympathetic voice. Yeah, right.

So, we all gathered in the largest music room. Jack was very kind to Cécile about her sprain, though, and said she mustn't worry and just do what she could. Yeah, right. Again.

Jennifer was all over Chris, of course. I think if he could have taken her weight whilst she clung on to his back like a great big baby monkey that would be her idea of reasonable proximity. From the casual way she greeted Marie-Camille it was clear she still didn't know she had a rival for Chris's affections. Chris extracted himself from her clutches and said hello. He had looked slightly nervous when he saw Marie-Camille arrive but just greeted her with a sly smile. I could see she was watching his every move.

Cécile went straight up on stage and asked Jack loads of questions; she kept him so busy he barely looked at me. After five minutes I needed to distract myself from this scene, so I went off to get a drink from the vending machines outside in the corridor. As I scrabbled for change in the bottom of my bag I felt a tap on my shoulder.

'Carrie.'

'Chris! Shouldn't you be getting ready or something?' I peered along the corridor behind him. 'Does your mummy know that you're out all by yourself?'

'Ha. Ha. Jen's had to collect dress stuff she forgot in the art room. I wanted to have a word with you.'

'With me? Why?'

'I wanted to apologise. You know, for being such a jerk. I know you were mad about that time with Jet, and I deserved it. I was a total idiot.'

I wasn't quite sure what to say. 'OK,' I began slowly. 'Yes, you were an idiot, but honestly it's not like it bothers me. We weren't even really going out, and let's face it, we're both much happier with other people now.'

He reached out and held on to my hand. From his screwed up eyes I guessed he was going for an intense look. 'But that's just it, Carrie. I'm not. When I see you with Jack it makes me so sad I messed up with you. That's why I flirted with your French girl. I wanted to make you jealous. I think we may still have a thing going on between us.'

I sighed. What a pile of crap. The only person Chris really has a 'thing' going on with is himself, and he couldn't bear that, just once, there was a girl who wasn't mad about him. He simply wanted to bring me back in line with his harem.

'Look, I know you have a compulsion to seduce any female with a pulse, and I'm sorry that my swift recovery to my senses offends you, but you've got two girls mad about you in a room very close to here, and I don't want any part of your stupid games. So shove off.' I tried to shake his hand off.

He hung on. 'Look, Carrie, if you still have feelings for me . . .'

And he started to drone on about us being a couple again and I told him my frank opinion of this which ended in me saying maturely, 'SO GO AWAY.'

'Come on, Carrie, just hear me out.'

'I don't want to hear you out! We both know this conversation is meaningless. But now you are here I will tell you that I am mad about the way you behaved with Marie-Camille. What about Jennifer? And you expect me to believe you when you say you're sorry about Jet? It was mean, mean, mean, to both of those girls.'

Even if Marie-Camille's behaviour with Tom had left a lot to be desired.

He released his hand and put it above my shoulder against the vending machine, temporarily blocking my escape.

'Listen, Carrie, Marie-Camille's a very cute girl, but she's going back to Paris in a few days. You cannot think that I'm seriously interested in her. It's you I'm interested in . . . you know we have something . . .'

But I wasn't listening any more because under his raised arm I could see Marie-Camille standing further down the corridor. And she had obviously heard what he had just said. She went white; turned around and ran back into the rehearsal room.

 MADDY'S TIP • • • • • • • • • • • • • • • • • •

Never tell yourself 'I'm not creative'. Everyone is naturally creative. Lots of us lose confidence in our abilities as we get older, or just feel other people are better than us, so stop trying. Picasso said that if we could draw as unselfconsciously as we did when we were four years old, we would all be geniuses. So be four again, when it didn't occur to you that you weren't a great artist. You were a creative being then and you are now. Think back to being smaller and what you liked doing. Dig deep and find that talent!

Chapter 17

Tuesday 6.00 a.m.

I cannot sleep.

I was too stressed to write any further last night. Tried to phone Jack all evening. His mobile was switched off. Left seven messages.

Just want to say first that Dr Jennings will be impressed by my tireless devotion to Chloe's dress considering the delicate state of my physical and mental well-being.

Not sure if I want to see another piece of material, pair of scissors or pincushion ever again either.

'Are you sure you still want to come back to mine?' Chloe had asked. As if I could stay in that music room with Marie-Camille's vibes of hatred bombarding me. Jennifer had sensed something was up as soon as Marie-Camille crashed back into the music room. Mind you it didn't take a genius; Rani said everyone stopped what they were doing and looked up and then I came running in after her, followed by the guiltiest-looking Chris.

Even Chloe had to say IT DID NOT LOOK GOOD.

Jack looked puzzled and came over to me. 'What's going on?'

'Yes, that's exactly what I would like to know,' Jennifer shouted. 'What *is* going on?'

Marie-Camille was staring at me expectantly.

'Absolutely nothing. Nothing at all,' I said and gave her a level look back.

She folded her arms, pouted and her neat little head turned meaningfully from Chris to me.

'What happened, Marie-Camille?' Jennifer's jaw clenched.

Marie-Camille gave a self-righteous sigh. 'It is not for me to say what I see. I prefer to say nuzzing.'

'Oh come on,' I gasped. 'This is stupid. Nothing happened!' I looked at Jack. Of course I just wanted to tell the truth but although I didn't give a hoot about exposing Chris for the slime ball *he* was, Jennifer *is* crazy about him and it would have been rather harsh to reveal in front of everyone what her stupid boyfriend had said to me. I'd explain it all to Jack later.

'Well if it's so stupid, Carrie, you won't mind telling us the details will you?' Jennifer was not a girl to let things go. Especially when it came to Chris. Who had re-gained his composure and was looking at me with an expression that bordered on amusement. Why was no one asking *him* any questions? Mind you, he could lie and smooth-talk his way out of anything.

A small voice said, 'Do we not have to go back to Chloe's house to begin the dress now?'

God bless Agathe.

'Yes, we do!' Chloe cried. 'Heavens, is that the time? We've got to get going. Come on.'

We hastily gathered our bags. Jennifer opened her mouth again.

'Honestly, Jen, nothing to say,' I jumped in. 'Silly, silly mis-understanding.'

I went up and kissed Jack goodbye and whispered, 'I'll call you later.'

'Sure,' he replied coolly.

Cécile sidled up. 'Come on, Jack, you play now, *n'est-ce pas?*' He walked back to the stage with her.

Marie-Camille glared daggers at me. 'Enjoy your sewing, Carrie,' she sneered.

I will be having a conversation about what happened with her as soon as she wakes up. I want to know what she said to Jennifer after I left. I need to be prepared. She was hiding in her room when I got back from Chloe's and I was too tired for a fight.

But I'm wide awake now.

5.30 p.m.

Frenchwomen are ruining my life. RUINING MY LIFE.

Tried to contact Jack all day and his mobile is still off. According to Tom, the rehearsal was abandoned due to artistic differences. Marie-Camille spoke animatedly to Jennifer who then spoke animatedly to Chris. Tom said he felt he should go so he left Jack talking quietly to Cécile. Thanks for telling me that, Tom. I feel so much better.

Had the row with Marie-Camille this morning. I waited till Mum went ahead to school because she had advised me very strongly against confronting Marie-Camille until I'd calmed down. She also said Marie-Camille was a 'troubled' girl. Ha! Not as troubled as I was.

When I heard her come out of her room I leaped out like a scary thing on a ghost train ride.

'Why did you do that?' I demanded.

'Do what?'

'Oh, come on. Make out that you saw something going on between me and Chris.'

She narrowed her eyes. 'I saw what I saw.'

'No, you didn't! You *thought* you saw something but you didn't. You really didn't.'

She blazed at me. 'I know what I saw and know what I *hear*.'

I sighed. 'I know you heard what Chris said about you, but honestly, Marie-Camille, I tried to warn you that he is not a nice person. You know I did. And he really isn't. I don't know why you're mad with me anyway. None of this was my fault. I told you *I am not interested in him*. You shouldn't be mad with me, you should be mad with him for leading you on.' And then I added, 'Except, honestly, he's not worth wasting time on. Just forget him.'

'Oh yes, you would like zis?' she spat. 'Would you not? The great Carrie, who everybody must love. You 'ave family who love you, zis not enough; you 'ave friends who love you, zis not enough; you 'ave boyfriend who love you, zis not enough; now you must 'ave every other boy too!'

'*What are you talking about?* Don't you see how crazy you sound? I am not interested in Chris. I never will be. Like I said, forget about him. Chris has a *girlfriend*. You know, like Tom has? Jennifer's a bit weird and scary but you never gave her a thought. You only thought about yourself, and what *you* wanted and when you couldn't get it, you thought you'd hurt other people. Do you know something? You want people to love you? Try being a hundred times nicer to them. See if that helps.'

She went pale. Then managed to contort her face into a smile.

'You 'ave always been jealous. Since the day I come 'ere. I understand, Carrie. Your little life is very small. Maybe one day you will leave 'ere and realise how boring your life is for me. With

Chris, I just try to make some amusement for me, this is all.'

'And what about Jennifer?'

'*You* cannot speak to me about Jennifer. I told Jennifer the truth about *you*.'

That didn't sound good.

'And what exactly is that?'

'I zink you know,' she hissed, and stormed downstairs.

And we haven't spoken since. Which was tricky in the art room this morning. But she got round it by saying, 'Susie, please tell Carrie she is sewing on those beads too close togezzer.' And I said, 'Susie, please tell Marie-Camille and I am trying to get them to match her eyes.' Etc, etc.

I did not speak to Cécile. Too humiliating to ask another girl what she spoke to your boyfriend about. Rani said she had asked her, but Cécile hadn't been very forthcoming.

If I thought Jennifer was going to let the events of the previous evening go, I was mistaken. She cornered me between a camel and a palm tree.

'I actually thought she was going to attack you,' Rani said cheerfully on our way downstairs after this encounter.

'She did poke my arm quite hard you know.' I was still in a state of outrage.

'Well, you *have* been "wildly jealous" of her ever since she started going out with Chris.' Rani grinned.

'Using, what did she say next? "Every cunning trick and wile you possess to lure him back",' Chloe continued.

'I didn't know I could lure,' I mumbled. 'I don't even know how to say it properly.'

'But Chris had told her to be sympathetic towards you, oh yes, that was the good bit,' Rani said, 'because you are "More to be pitied than despised".'

They both collapsed into giggles.

'It's not funny you know – Jack still isn't answering my calls.'

He is definitely avoiding me. As is Chris – who will get more than a finger jabbing at his arm when I get hold of him.

I am going round to Rani's now. Her mum is taking us to Chloe's for more work on the dress. Luckily the French girls have been taken to see a concert so I am spared seeing Marie-Camille.

9.45 p.m.

Have heard from Jack! At last. I am in heaven.

He called just as I was going out to Chloe's. 'Got your messages. Thanks.'

'Why has it taken you so long to get back to me? Why haven't you answered my calls?' (Very unimpressive dog-person stuff there, I'm sad to report.)

'I'm sorry – you know, everyone saying different things. Scared of making a fool of myself – very dumb. You have to admit it did look a bit weird. But I have just had a call from Jennifer – she must have got my number from Chris – asking me to restrain your passion for her boyfriend, and I suddenly realised how stupid this all is. I know that you were telling the truth; you are the world's worst liar and I trust you. Coupled with the fact I credit you with more brains than to like that prat. I'm sorry I even let myself doubt you for a minute. Forgive me?'

Forgive him! I wanted to climb down the phone and hug him for ever.

'Of course. But if you could just always remember from now

on what a lovely, kind, truthful person I am you will save yourself a lot of stress in the future.'

'I'll try to remember that.'

'Good.'

And then I desperately wanted to ask him about his conversation with Cécile, but even I realised that this might best be left to another time.

I am positively delirious with relief.

Jack still likes me. Chloe's dress is going to be ready on time. Marie-Camille is still out at the concert.

Apart from hearing Ned crooning, *'I closed my eyes, drew back the curtain,'* as he went past on the way to the bathroom, my life is brilliant.

 RANI'S TIP ● ● ● ● ● ● ● ● ● ● ● ● ● ● ● ● ● ● ●

If you want to apply two coats of mascara, the secret to avoid a clumpy mess is to not let the first coat dry before you apply the second. To avoid lumpy lashes, change your mascara at least every three months and wipe the wand on a tissue before applying.

Chapter 18

Wednesday 8.15 a.m.

On the bus.

Chloe is bringing her dress in today. Last night Rani and I lugged her mum's sewing machine up the stairs to her flat with a passable impersonation of the Chuckle Brothers. Those machines are much heavier than you would think.

We were surprised to see Agathe lying on the sofa in Chloe's flat with a flannel on her forehead.

'Oh God – you're not getting the bug,' I gasped.

'She's not feeling well at all,' Chloe's mum fussed. 'Not well enough to go out to the play all the exchanges are going out to anyway. I'm wondering if I should stay in tonight.'

Jim's face fell. He was standing at the door with his friend Vicky ready to be taken to the film he's been going on about for weeks.

'Please, go,' Agathe whispered. 'I will be OK. I 'ave the girls to care for me.'

'Go on, Mum,' Chloe urged. 'We'll be fine, really.'

As soon as Chloe's mum had left, Agathe rose from the sofa like a mummy from the tomb in a horror film. She gave us all a grin.

'I thought you were ill!' Rani shrieked.

'*Non*,' Agathe looked mischievous. '*Non*, I am pretending. The play is not important. But the dress, it is. And you never manage without me.'

And this was true. Yesterday she had cut out the pattern and material and pinned everything together. It would have taken us days to get that far.

Rani nodded next to me. 'Let's get on with it then,' she said, rubbing her hands together briskly.

'Ooh, you're very assertive today, Rani. I'm impressed.'

'Carrie, you have no idea how assertive I've been today. I decided to speak to Kenny.'

'What about?' I looked at her and gasped. 'Not the lippy-clinch situation?

'Yes indeed.'

'So you just called him up and said you wanted to discuss your relationship?'

'Yup, just wanted to get it all sorted, once and for all.'

'So what did you both decide?'

'After a long discussion he decided to agree with me that Manon and Océane *are* pond life and that he is now my *boy* best friend.'

'What!'

'He's my *boy* best friend. And I'm his *girl* best friend.'

'And you're both happy with that are you?'

'Do you know something, Carrie? I really think we are. I hated being awkward with him. It meant we didn't have any laughs because we were always both so tense. Sounds crazy but we haven't had so much fun talking together for ages.'

I love Rani. She's so brave. 'Well, I envy you,' I sighed wistfully. 'At least you don't have to worry about him being poached by Cécile.'

Rani frowned. 'Let it go, Carrie. I think you've got it wrong about Cécile liking Jack. The only thing she seems to think about is Lucy Kell coming to judge her dress. And it has meant her parents didn't cancel coming up from London. I am dreading it. Dad will be pumping them for tips on how to get the best out of your daughter.'

'You make it sound like he's growing a prize leek.'

'That's what it feels like sometimes,' she said mournfully.

'Poor you, but I can't believe her parents would have considered not coming to the show just because no one famous was going to be the judge.'

'Are you kidding?' Rani squeaked. 'Cécile says there's no way they'd bother unless her triumph was going to be MEGA. Apparently in her family small triumphs aren't worth diddly squat.'

No – only big ones like trying to steal *my boyfriend*. And then I checked myself for being mean. Perhaps I had been wrong about her. Like Jennifer was wrong about me. After all she was always really nice to Agathe whereas most of the others ignored her completely.

I must try to be a better person.

6.30 p.m.

Day started well.

Jack came into school and met me off the bus and we had a delicious kiss to make up. Huzzah!

Chloe's dress made quite a stir in the art room. Although it wasn't finished yet, you could see the basic structure of it clearly. Half black, half white. When the huge floor-length sash was added and the hundreds of thin torn strips of fabric were sewn all over it was going to be gorgeous. When you moved it would be like a Pop Art cornfield rippling. We just needed a few more hours on the art room sewing machine. Everyone gathered round.

'Incredible!' Katia, swathed in a huge yellow jumper, gasped. 'It's very fun, *n'est-ce pas?*'

Jennifer looked at the dress and pursed her lips, sneering at us. 'It's hardly conventional, is it?' Any project that I was involved in was *never* going to get her approval.

Rani crossed her arms. 'No one said it had to be conventional. It can be just ridiculously pretty and fun to wear – which it will be when it's finished.'

Cécile who had gone over every bit of it with Marie-Camille said she thought it was very 'charming'.

Marie-Camille remained defiantly unimpressed. Safe to say relations were still cool between us. She waved her hands over it. 'It's a crazy design. It is too bizarre . . .'

'Yes, but that's what people thought about Lucy Kell at first. And what about Vivienne Westwood?'

Cécile was still examining the dress. 'I worry that you may not 'ave enough time for the finishing. Did not Madame Crowe say all the dresses must be ready by Thursday evening? It is Wednesday now. I worry you 'ave not the hours for all the detail.'

This was disturbingly true.

'We're still hoping we might do it,' Chloe said.

Marie-Camille suddenly let out an exasperated sigh. 'Pah! It is too late. I zink the dress is never ready, it cannot be finished. Tonight is the show wiz Ned. You 'ave not enough time. YOU WON'T DO IT.'

And she stormed out.

'Well!' Rani whistled. '*She's* not a happy bunny, is she?'

'She's right though. We have got *Joseph* tonight. And lessons all day with no free periods.' I sighed. Curse Ned and his coat of many colours. Talking of which . . . time to go.

10.30 p.m.

The show is over. Ned was not the total embarrassment I feared. It pains me say it, but he was really rather good. At least, everyone who stood up at the end and cheered and clapped thought so. Surprisingly, I appeared to be one of them.

After the show, Rani, Chloe, Maddy and I stood outside in the cool night air waiting for Mum. Marie-Camille wandered over with Cécile and Manon.

'Ned is very good I zink.' Cécile opened the conversation.

'Good! He was brilliant!' Rani enthused.

'Maybe it make you feel less sad about the dress?' Manon's eyes glinted.

'What do you mean?'

'You cannot finish the dress because of the ze show, but ze show was *super*.'

I caught Chloe's eye. 'Oh, didn't we say? The dress is finished.'

Three pairs of French eyes opened wide.

'But, but 'ow?' Marie-Camille gasped.

'Well, you'll laugh. It's quite a funny story,' Rani said. 'You see, this afternoon, our regular teacher was away. So we had the large romantic-novel-reading, sweet-eating, supply teacher.' She looked at the girls' bemused faces. 'Never mind. Anyway, Carrie immediately went up and said she needed to go to the loo. She dashed up to the art room where she found it empty as Mrs Crowe had gone on the same course as Miss Gwatkins.' She came down and told romantic-novel reader that Mrs McGuy needed to see her, Chloe and me immediately. Toffee-muncher waved us off. Hey presto! Two hours uninterrupted in the art room. Isn't that just the luckiest thing?'

'Did no one find out?' Manon asked.

'Not till the end of the day. Someone told Mrs McGuy we left a lesson. I suspect Jennifer. But by then we had done it. We *do* all have Friday lunchtime detention. But it was so worth it.'

Cécile's good manners kicked in immediately. 'But this is great news. Congratulations.'

'It shall be very interesting to see zis dress now it is finished,' Marie-Camille said evenly. 'Very interesting.'

 CARRIE'S TIP ● ● ● ● ● ● ● ● ● ● ● ● ● ● ●

Lighting in your room is important. Unlike in a theatre, natural light is important. Have your make-up mirror by a window to get the best of the natural daylight. I can't count the number of times I've thought I've done a good job and then caught my reflection in a mirror under bright shop lighting and got a shock. That blob of concealer that I thought I had smudged in properly and the blusher that looked just the right colour by the dim glow of my bedside table lamp, so wasn't.

Chapter 19

On bus.

Ned's Joseph is the talk of the bus. 'Sensitive and heartfelt performance,' Sasha said to him. And she wasn't being sarcastic. Even Jet told him it wasn't bad. Feel grudging sense of relief he did not shame me totally, and yes, some pride. And further relief that they're thinking of *Grease* next, which at least requires more clothes.

Marie-Camille stopped me on the landing this morning. (I still can't get over the fact people actually *wear* cashmere dressing gowns.)

'You will make ze show a joke wiz Chloe's dress . . .'

'Why don't you wait till you see it finished?'

'I do not 'ave to. I know it.'

'No, you don't.'

'Yes, I *do*.'

'*Do* not.' Etc, etc.

I *wish* I'd had Agathe as my exchange. Rani wishes she'd had Agathe too. Another thing I wish is that Rani would stop leaning on me. She's making my writing go wobbly. Rani is depressed this morning. It's Cécile's parents; they will soon be here. She said her dad spoke to Cécile's dad on the phone last night and it was clear the conversation revolved around the fabulousness that was Cécile. Her dad kept nodding and saying, 'Yes, I *do* think in a competitive world one has to give one's child every opportunity to develop new skills.' And giving Rani *'You see?'* looks the whole way through. 'Mmm . . . yes. Always top in class and her project is going to be the best blah, blah, blah. Marvellous.' Rani said even Cécile had gone rather quiet and overwhelmed by it all. At breakfast, Rani got a huge lecture from her dad about the importance of success and striving to do well in all things.

'He said that he feels he should follow their example and push me more,' moaned Rani.

'Push you *more*? I think I should let him know what happens if you push people too far.'

'What?'

'What? Well, er . . . OK, if you push people too far they . . .'

'Yes? They what? This could be useful to me in my argument, Carrie.'

'Have nervous breakdowns? Shoplift? Streak down the high street?'

'God, Carrie, that is pitiful. Is that the best you can do in my hour of need? What would Dr Jennings say?'

We looked at each other. We both knew where this was going to end. Rani, *MENTAL about MATHS,* and no more hot chocolate at The Coffee Bean.

On a positive note, as Cécile passed us to go and take her seat, she said she was really looking forward to seeing Chloe's finished dress. I have decided my paranoia about her was unjustified. Jack and I are meeting around school at every opportunity. We have decided on a total trust pact.

Actually there is quite a buzz about the dress on the bus this morning too. Everyone is curious about it. They'll have to wait as there's going to be a special assembly for the French girls about their English projects. But afterwards I think there will be a stampede to the art room to see the finished article.

9.00 p.m.

My hands are an interesting combination of red and magenta. We have been dyeing banners. They are going to look fantastic against the black and white dresses. It's been hard work getting it done in breaks and at lunchtimes, but so worth it.

Chloe hung her dress up next to the others when we got in this morning.

Katia foolishly cried, 'I zink you might win wiz zis!' In front of everyone. Jennifer gave her a furious glare. Which Katia returned with a huge grin. Katia doesn't take any nonsense from Jennifer.

I spotted Chris at lunch, first time out of hiding but he has to come in for exams. He was standing in the queue with his weasely mate Jonny Poynton. Rani used to have a crush on him but not any more. We were waiting for Kenny and Jack to join us. Chris saw me watching and gave a little wave. That did it.

I put my knife and fork down. 'I'm going to have a word with him.'

Rani's hand shot out. 'Please, please don't. He isn't worth it.'

Chloe nodded her head vigorously but I was already scrambling off the bench.

'He has besmirched my name. And I will not have it! I will not have my name being besmirched all over school. Especially by a person such as he.' (We had just come out of a Shakespeare class.)

Maddy attempted a last desperate grab at my shirt, but I was too quick for her and marched over.

'Oi, you,' I said. Chris turned and his tan faded a shade. 'I want to talk to you.'

He looked up and down the queue. 'What, here?'

'Here if you like. I'm happy to have to say what I want to say here, I'm not fussed. Shall I begin?'

'Er, no.' He was obviously anxious Jennifer was going to appear. 'Let's go outside for a minute.'

'You are kidding! I'm not going anywhere "outside" with you. Just get out of the line.'

And still carrying his empty tray we went and stood next to a display screen. I could see Rani standing on the bench in the distance, making slashing motions across her neck and pointing frantically as we disappeared round the other side of it. But I was on a mission and not to be stopped. My hands were on my hips by now.

'Listen, Chris, if you ever, *ever* approach me again with the sort of crap you came out with the other evening I will not be responsible for my actions. You *know* I couldn't be less interested in you. You said it made you "sad" to see me with Jack Harper. Well you *should* be sad, because you must realise he's a million times more interesting and attractive to me than you ever were, *or ever will be*. Is that clear? And another thing, I want you to know that far from *"wanting you back"*, I think you're stupid, vain and boring. And the last person on earth to whom I would say – now what did you tell Jennifer I said – *please* let's get back together; you know I'm still mad about you. I'm *begging* you.' I put my hands together like I was pleading to give it more effect.

I felt a hand on my shoulder. 'Carrie, Carrie, this has *got* to stop.' There was a pause. 'You've *got* to let go.' It was Jennifer. She didn't look angry. Oh no. She looked *sorry for me*. I wasn't sure which was worse.

Chris saw his chance and shook his head from side to side and tut-tutted in an understanding way. He took her arm. 'Come on Jennifer, best we go.' He turned to me. 'Sorry, Carrie, but it's like I said, it's not going to happen.'

I stood rooted to the spot in disbelief. Then I put my head in my hands to groan. I realised someone was standing next to me. It was Jack. Brilliant. He was looking serious.

'Thought you'd give it another try did you?'

Oh God. Here we go again.

I put my hands down and looked at him.

'What were you talking about?' he said, jerking his head in the direction Chris had just gone. 'Thought you'd have another try with him, did you?'

'No! The opposite! I know it might have looked a bit, er . . . weird, but I was actually letting him know how angry I was about the other evening. Because it messed with *our* relationship.'

'So that must be why you said,' he put on a wheedling voice, '"Please let's get back together; you know I'm still mad about you. I'm *begging* you." That's being angry with someone is it?'

Oh no.

'Jack, I didn't say that. Well, I did, but not in the way you thought. I was saying what *he* said I said . . .'

Jack interrupted me. 'The thing is Carrie, you know we made a pact about trust?'

'Mmm.' Oh God, please, please, don't finish with me. I will never be happy again. Ever. My head drooped.

'I thought we'd sorted all this out. I thought we were beyond this, and now I hear that conversation, what am I am supposed to think?'

'If you'd only heard the whole thing you would have known what I really said!' I wailed desperately.

'Heard the whole thing? I trusted you, Carrie. Do you honestly think that I would abuse that trust by spotting you haul Chris out of the line, following you across the dining hall, watching you disappear behind a screen and then eavesdropping on your whole conversation?'

I lifted my head. I felt a faint stirring of hope. I looked up into his eyes. 'Yes?'

'Correct.' He smiled. 'Sometimes this "trust" thing is overrated.'

'You . . . you . . . pig!' I said and made some feeble flailing motions at his chest.

I stopped suddenly. I'd thought of something else.

'OK, Jack, tell me this, why didn't you stop Jennifer?'

He screwed up his nose.

'I don't know, Carrie, I just couldn't. It was so obviously going to be such pure comedy gold.'

'At my expense!'

'Sorry.'

'You're not sorry really, are you?'

'No. Not really.'

I love him.

CHLOE'S TIP ••••••••••••••••••••

Celebrate feeling good, or cheer yourself up by wearing some big costume jewellery. Charity shops often sell good original pieces that no one else will have and you can pick something up very cheaply. If you invest in some jewellery wire (they sell it in the haberdasher's in big department stores or craft shops) you can dismantle broken necklaces, etc, and use the beads, pearls or stones to make your own creations.

Chapter 20

Friday 1.00 p.m.

I am writing this in my lunchtime detention. I wouldn't normally risk writing my diary under the cold vulture eyes of Mrs McG. But something so horrible has happened I don't care about getting caught. I should never get happy. Something always happens to ruin it.

After registration and assembly everyone scrambled up to the art room for a final look at the dresses before the show this afternoon.

And there was Chloe's dress, hanging alongside all the others. At first we couldn't understand what had happened. Chloe was kneeling down, picking up pieces of black and white material from the floor, confused.

It was Katia who held out a handful and said in a hushed voice, 'Someone 'ave cut your dress, Chloe.'

Chloe slowly turned the dress round. She uttered a small cry. Someone had made a rip at the neckline and hacked all around the bottom with crude slashes and chops.

Everyone stood around, not knowing what to do.

'It's just ruined,' Chloe whispered, spreading it out between her fingers. She was fighting back tears. 'But why? I can't understand who would do this.'

But I had a good idea.

Mrs Crowe bustled her way to the front of the crowd. She was horrified. 'I just can't understand it. No one has been in here this morning.'

'Someone *has* been in though, haven't they?' I said. 'They could easily have dashed up here before registration. It would only have taken a few minutes.'

I couldn't help staring at Marie-Camille. I wasn't the only one. No one said anything but she saw everyone's eyes on her.

'Come on, girls, no one is accusing anyone. I would hope that if anyone knows something about this then they would tell me. I'm so sorry, especially for you, Chloe. I know how hard you've worked to get this ready in time. This must be a terrible blow. In the circumstances I am prepared to bend the rules and let you work on this today. Perhaps you can try to repair the damage as best you can.' She ran her hands through the tattered hem.

But we knew it was impossible. We had this Friday lunchtime detention. We couldn't get out of it. We couldn't skive off lessons – after yesterday, every teacher in the school was watching us like a hawk. Including Mum.

I only have one consolation: that I will soon be able to prove who cut the dress.

As soon as I got into our first lesson – maths – I sat down next to Maddy and wrote her a note: *Chloe's dress slashed. Must have been done this morning before register. Chloe devastated. All devastated.*

She read it and turned to me, appalled. She folded over my note, scribbled frantically and passed it back: *I was in art room this morning! Went to take photos before register as it was the last morning before the show. Wanted to shoot finished dresses all hanging up together. Went into teacher's cupboard afterwards to take shots of empty rolls of material. Heard someone outside.*

So you saw who did it?! I scrawled frantically.

NO! she wrote. *Thought it was someone doing last minute adjustments to dress. So carried on taking photos in cupboard. Bell for register rang. Knocked over pot of beads as I came out of cupboard. They ran off. Took photo though. Don't know why – automatic reaction. Don't think it will be helpful but will develop it this afternoon.*

Didn't you notice the dress had been damaged? I asked.

She passed back her reply. *NO!!!!! Thought person I tried to take photo of was just running because, like me, late for register. Was in such hurry didn't look at dresses again. Sorry – feel so bad.*

So we have to wait till later this afternoon. I am going to encourage her to get a digital camera.

2.00 p.m.

Detention is finished. Chloe cried quietly the whole way through. I couldn't bear it. She would not get the chance to show her design in front of her idol. Even though she would never have said it, being part of Cécile's team just wouldn't be the same.

I'm in the big changing room for the fashion show. It starts at three p.m. I am meeting Cara in the lighting box at two forty-five p.m. I must not be late. Found it so hard to care any more, but I had to tell myself that this show wasn't just about Chloe's dress. The excited shrieking and yelling going on around me told me that this was an important day for lots of people.

The rehearsal room backstage has been separated along one wall with display screens, a bit like stables. On the other side of the display screens, the room is full of clothes and make-up and shoes and hysterical girls. I could see Chloe and Rani helping Cécile get ready from where I sat. It just wasn't fair. But at least I still had hope that Maddy's photo would shed some light on who had ruined Chloe's dream.

'Carrie?' Maddy's face popped over the screen.

My heart jumped, but she shook her head.

'Sorry, Carrie. I developed it, but you can only see a blurry hand in the corner disappearing around the door. You couldn't possibly tell who it was. I could try to blow it up but I'm not sure that would really tell us any more.'

It was so disappointing.

'Don't worry, Maddy, thanks so much for trying. You're a star.'

'Just wish it could have been more helpful.'

Marie-Camille hadn't appeared yet. I wondered what must be going through *her* mind now. It was Susie who brought her dress down from the art room. I couldn't bear to go up there again. It is very elegant, long black satin with plunging back and beads embroidered around the bodice and down the back of the skirt. In spite of everything I can't help feeling proud of all the work we put into it.

'Where on earth is Katia?' Jennifer shrieked in the next-door booth. 'I haven't seen her since lunchtime! What does she think she's doing? She promised she'd bring the dress down.'

''Ere it is!' cried Katia, almost hidden by the frills on the dress she was carrying. If a celebrity in a ballroom dancing competition had decided to go a bit over the top on her wedding day, she need have looked no further.

'I put it on now?'

Jennifer pretended to look bored – she had never really got

over not being the model. Mind you, making anyone wear that dress was surely revenge enough. Jennifer looked over the screen. 'You OK, Carrie?' Since yesterday she now spoke to me as if I was not quite sane. I ignored her.

Rani and Chloe came over. 'Have you seen Agathe?'

'Mmm. She was in the art room – being secretive in a corner with Katia and Fleur. What's going on there?'

'I've no —' But I stopped talking because Marie-Camille had arrived.

She looked as if she was about to say something when, 'TARAAA!' We all jumped. Fleur and Agathe leaped in front of us, holding a bundle of black and white fabric. Katia, now dressed, came hurtling over, scattering girls, shoes and chairs in her wake.

'We mend ze dress!' she yelled.

'What?' Chloe was watching them unravel the material.

'We mend your dress. Agathe show us what to do. We mend it.'

Sure enough all the jagged and slashed material at the bottom had been cut off and the skirt beautifully re-hemmed. The rip at the top had been carefully stitched back together. You would never have known that there had been anything wrong with it.

'You see only bottom and little of top is cut. Ze rest is OK. We mend it.'

Chloe was running her fingers over the work. 'But this is fantastic. How on earth did you find the time?'

'We go to art room. No one zere. We supposed to go to watch film, to keep us busy till show. But we do not go. We stay in art room. When people start to come in to get dress we just say we got zere little bit early.'

'You skived, Agathe!'

'Yes, I skive!'

Rani was now looking at the dress. 'There is just a teensy-weensy problem here.'

Chloe nodded. 'I know.'

'It's way too small for you now.'

Everyone looked at Rani. 'We zink,' Fleur began. 'We zink, Rani is veree small person.'

Rani looked agonised. '*Don't* look at me. You know I'm doing hair and make-up for everyone all evening. I can't take time off to do myself and go down a catwalk. I'm already hopelessly behind. You know I would – but I *can't* let everyone else in the show down. Not now I've said I'll do it. But of course there is an obvious alternative.'

We all turned to Agathe. She began to wring her hands.

'No, please, not me. I could not. I could not . . .' But Rani was already pressing the dress up against her. 'Go and try it *on* at least.' She thrust it in her hands.

With an agonised look, Agathe took the dress. 'I will change in the *toilettes* if you please.' And she left the room.

'Better go after her,' Rani said, 'in case she changes her mind.' And she and Chloe disappeared a while ago.

 MADDY'S TIP ••••••••••••••••••••

Count to five, or preferably take five minutes, before yelling at anyone or saying something when angry. If you can manage to do it, it's a skill you will never regret having learned. I'm still working on it, but I'm getting there.

Chapter 21

Friday 11.05 p.m.

Cannot possibly sleep. Not at all tired.

I passed Rani and Chloe on my way to Cara. They were banging on the door in the girls' toilets.

'I promise you, you will look sensational,' Rani soothed. She raised her eyebrows at me and pointed to the toilet door.

'Bit of last minute nerves,' Chloe whispered. I couldn't linger.

Cara greeted me with a shake of her fist. 'About time. Sit down and get yourself organised.'

A head immediately peered round the door. 'She's here, you know. I've seen her, sitting in the front row.' It was Sasha, toddling past in her Morticia Addams outfit. Very narrow at the ankle region.

'Who's here?' I asked, confused.

'Lucy blimmin' Kell, that's who. Who d'ya think?'

And there she was, sitting next to Mum in the front row. She was tall and angular with sleek, dark hair pulled back into an elegant chignon. Mum, less tall, round, with a halo of frizz. Lucy Kell in long, wide silk trousers and funky tuxedo worn with stylish huge frilled lace shirt. Mum, a symphony in navy polyester. Sitting close by, next to Rani's mum and dad was a tall, well-dressed couple; they were watching the stage expectantly. I guessed they must be Cécile's parents. Poor Rani.

'Carrie?'

Ned's head had popped round the door of the lighting box.

'What are you doing here?' I hissed at him.

'I heard about, you know, what happened to Chloe's dress . . .'

'Really? I didn't know you cared, but if you're so concerned I can tell you that the dress has been saved.' I turned to look at Cara. 'Though I still can't believe anyone would do something like that. And then act as if she knows nothing at all.'

'She? Who's she?' Ned asked.

I pursed my lips together. Ned went on.

'Because if you mean Marie-Camille, she came straight to my form room as soon as she got off the bus to help me with my French conversation. We had a big test today and she said my accent was awful. She was with me until the bell rang.'

I took my hands off the lighting controls. 'She did?'

'She did. Well, good luck with the show,' he said, and shot off. A storm of confusion whirled in my mind.

'Come on.' Cara gave me a shove. 'No time to think about that now, Carrie. We've got a show to do. I'm going to dim the lights.'

Then I switched on the spotlight.

Mrs Crowe appeared tentatively from behind a magenta banner, sidled into the pool of light and gave a speech about the success of the project and how it had brought everyone together. When she finished, everyone gave her a huge round of applause. She looked like a rabbit caught in the headlights. But a pleased rabbit.

Then the music began to crash around the hall and Lucy Kell got out her notebook. It was time for the main event.

There were lots of highlights. Jet, for instance: one's eye was inevitably drawn to her skin – a curious shade of orange, unknown in the natural world – due to the lack of dress. What there was of it was slit all the way up to the thigh (almost the waist really, some said). Members of the audience were in dispute afterwards if a thong was in evidence or not. The audience was in no dispute about evidence of Jet's ample boobs. They were falling out all over the place. Hair and make-up not done by Rani, but by the Barbie School of Beauty.

I tried to see Rani's dad's expression when Sarah Li's Puritan dress came on; it certainly will be invaluable in History Alive! Club for years to come.

Katia's frothy concoction was in stark contrast to Jackie's *Doctor Who* number – the silver foil star on her head worked well with the matching bra. Then Marie-Camille came on in her dress. I had to admit it was stunning – so sophisticated and grown-up. I did feel proud of all the hard work we had put into making it. Even if we had been practically forced at gunpoint. She had driven us mad but she *had* got us to create something very Parisian. Then it was Cécile's turn; with her blonde hair piled up on her head and her French tan against the white satin, she looked like a Greek goddess. She had a filigree wire of silver stars around her head and thin strappy silver sandals. Her parents clapped so hard even Rani's dad looked startled.

As the models came and went, the dresses showed up as spectacularly as I had hoped against the bright red and magenta banners. And then it came to the last entry. Chloe's dress. Agathe came on to the catwalk. The audience did not seem to recognise her at first. She was in a pair of Rani's black platform shoes. Her hair was tied up with black strips of torn fabric, a single black strip was around her neck. She had kohl around her eyes, making them look huge, and a scarlet Cupid's-bow mouth. She looked like a strange but beautiful doll. The thin strips of black and white fabric echoed her movements as she posed at the end, first one way, then the other, and then with a saucy twirl she sashayed back down the runway.

The music crescendoed into the finale. The audience stood up and cheered and everyone came out on to the stage. Cara and I handed the lights over to Mr Goodge and went down to be with everyone who had worked on the dresses. It was so exciting with the dresses swirling black and white around us. I couldn't help noticing Jennifer shoving a startled Katia through to the front, pushing her next to Marie-Camille and Cécile.

When everyone had finished clapping, Madame Debas made a small speech about what an exhilarating experience we'd all had and what a collaborative operation it had been to get these designs prepared. 'And we are honoured to have as our judge tonight one of the most talented and famous of Great Britain's designers . . . Miss Lucy Kell!'

Everyone went crazy. Especially Chloe.

Mum led her to the front of the catwalk. Maddy was frantically taking photos.

'Wasn't that just amazing!' Miss Kell began to much cheering. 'When I think of the short time that you've had to put this together I am overwhelmed by the high standard of your designs. I truly am. They included elements of, er . . . unusual daring,' (Jet hoisted a boob back in place and beamed) 'wild originality and impressive sophistication. I would also like to praise the stylists and the set designers – all of which were crucial elements in making the show such a success.'

I grinned at Rani.

'I know every dress was the result of hard work by the teams including both French and English girls.' Chloe squeezed Agathe's hand. 'And that is what this project was all about: people working together, helping each other, to make something special. And that means, *everyone* here is a winner.'

More cheering.

'But I do have to chose one design. As you know, the prize will be a day in my studio. As I have one both in London and Paris, both the French and British members of the winning team will be able to visit one or the other. The standard was so high, with some surprisingly sophisticated ideas for such young designers.'

Marie-Camille and Cécile smiled. It was obvious she was talking about their designs.

'There was elegant use of fabrics and decoration, and excellent workmanship. It is clear that some of you have already got first-hand knowledge and understanding of the world of the best fashion designers . . .'

I felt Chloe take a step back. She knew Lucy Kell wasn't talking about her. She bit her lip. I gave her free hand a consoling squeeze.

'It's OK,' she whispered, forcing a smile. 'It only mattered that she saw it, and at least that happened. That's the main thing.'

'In the final analysis, however,' Lucy Kell continued, 'I have given the prize to the dress that showed the most originality and flair and which showed the most promise and talent in its designer. And that was the dress of the team led by Chloe Simmonds. Congratulations, Chloe! A wonderful creation!'

Shrieking, jumping up and down and crying broke out. Chloe's mum came up on stage to give her a hug and to thank Agathe for being such a great model, and Rani for making

Agathe look so extraordinary and me for giving them such a stunning setting to show them in. Katia and Fleur were dancing round and round, which was dangerous as Katia's skirt was like a tornado crossing the prairie of the stage. Mum put a restraining hand on her shoulder before someone was knocked off into the front row.

'Quiet, quiet,' she called out. Then she made her teacher calming noises and order was restored. She gestured Chloe forward.

Chloe suddenly turned into a sheepdog, and rounded up Agathe, Fleur, Katia, Rani and me and herded us towards the front of the stage.

'Goodness,' Lucy Kell laughed. 'It *was* a team effort!'

'Can they all come to the studios?' Chloe asked anxiously. 'They were all part of it.'

'Of course!'

'But honestly, we only helped make it,' I gushed. 'It was totally her design.'

Lucy Kell looked at Chloe. 'Well, it was a seriously impressive one. When you come to the studio we need to talk about you doing some work experience there when you are older.'

Chloe burst into tears.

'Oh my goodness, Chloe.' She laughed. 'You don't have to do it if you don't want to!'

'She does, she does!' Rani cried, putting her arm around her. 'It's just that it's been rather an emotional rollercoaster of a day for Chloe; she didn't think the dress was going to be able to be shown, and now this.'

But Chloe had collected herself. 'Thank you so much, you really have no idea how much this means.'

'Oh, but I do.' Lucy Kell smiled. 'I do; I was once just like you. Keep going. You've got talent, Chloe. Work hard and amazing things can happen.'

I love Lucy Kell.

 RANI'S TIP • • • • • • • • • • • • • • • • • •

If you are small, don't be embarrassed about going into children's departments for clothes and shoes. Some of the stuff now is amazing and it's cheaper too. If people ask where you got it, just look a little vague and say you can't remember. And hope they don't have a younger sister.

Chapter 22

Saturday 9.35 p.m.

They've gone.

The coach left at midday. The car park felt strangely quiet after the chaos of parents, girls and teachers all milling around trying to say goodbye to everyone all at once.

Chloe and Rani came back here. We were all sitting squashed on my bed, eating cheese and pickle sandwiches. Tuna and mayo is so over.

'It's going to be so sad without them,' Chloe sighed. Agathe had cried her eyes out saying goodbye.

'No more art room first thing,' Rani said, nodding.

'No more Jennifer saying, "Katia, have you ever *tried* wearing a skirt?"' I added.

'Is she still treating you like you've escaped from a home for the bewildered?' Rani queried.

'Yup. I don't mind. Better than living in fear of another poke in the arm.'

'No more Mrs McGuy having a fit at Mam'selle Nanty's outfits every morning.' Chloe sounded wistful. 'We'll miss them.'

The doorbell went. It was Maddy.

'I've got something to show you.' She was hopping about on the doorstep waving an envelope.

'What is it?'

'Tell you when we're all together.'

Rani had got up to nose around my room so Maddy took her place on the bed.

'Look at this.' She produced a large photograph out of the envelope.

We all looked at her enquiringly.

'Don't you see? It's the photo I took, of the hand disappearing out of the art room.'

'But Carrie said you couldn't make out who it was,' Rani said with a frown.

'You couldn't! But this morning I was in the dark room at home, developing prints of the show and I thought, "What the hell, I'll blow it up and see if anything else comes up".'

'And did it?' Chloe asked.

'See for yourself.' She brandished the grainy black and white photograph. Round the wrist you could now quite clearly see a delicate gold charm bracelet.

I couldn't believe my eyes.

'Cécile!' Rani gasped.

'I know.' Maddy nodded. 'Cécile. How weird is that? Why would *she* do it?'

Rani looked thoughtful. 'You know, if you had seen the scene that went on at our house last night you might understand it more. My dad asked her parents back for a drink after the show and her dad did nothing but quiz Cécile. "What happened? What happened? This would never happen with your sister." He was furious with her.'

'Seriously!' Chloe was shocked.

'Then her mum began: "I can't believe that we have come all the way from London for you to *let yourself down* in front of everybody".'

'That's horrible,' I said.

'Actually, there's another thing.'

We all looked at Chloe.

'When I was helping Agathe pack last night I was puzzled because I found two English projects. You know Cécile won the prize for best one?'

We all nodded. No surprise there. Agathe's had been the runner up.

'I asked Agathe why on earth she'd write two. She just muttered something about one not being very good and having to do it again. But I think I understand now. She did one for Cécile. And Cécile just copied it out. I suspect Agathe does a lot of Cécile's work.'

'But why?' I asked.

'Because Agathe's very insecure and shy, and Cécile is so cool and popular. When Agathe won the scholarship to that posh school I expect she couldn't believe it when someone like Cécile wanted to be her friend.'

'Especially since it's full of girls like Marie-Camille who didn't want anything to do with her.'

'And Cécile saw her opportunity. Someone to help her stay at the top of the class.'

'But I think things will change now. Agathe's gained so much confidence by being here, and all the girls in her class have seen how talented she is. And then modelling the winning dress. She's been spending more time with Fleur and Katia recently – I think they're going to end up being good friends to her.'

'What about Cécile though?'

'You can't keep a pretence up for ever,' Maddy said with feeling.

'I think you need to tell your mum about this, Carrie.' She tapped the photo.

'But she'll tell Cécile's parents!'

'Exactly. It will be horrible but it's the only way they might realise what they are doing to her. Pushing her all the time and expecting her to be just like her sister. The strain on her must be terrible. I expect in a strange way it will be a relief. Otherwise who knows what Cécile might do next?'

'What's this?' It was Rani. She had discovered a package under my dressing table, beautifully wrapped in an elegant brown bag.

'I don't know.' I was puzzled. 'Pass it over. I hope it's not something Marie-Camille forgot – Mum said she got a parcel sent over by express delivery this morning. Which is weird considering it was her last day. She didn't need any more stuff. We barely got it all in the car as it was.' I pulled out a card from the bag. 'It's for me! From Marie-Camille.'

'Open it then!' Rani urged.

I pulled the parcel out of the bag and unwrapped the tissue. Inside was a drawstring cloth bag.

'Oh my God. Look at the name on it!' Chloe gasped.

Inside the cloth bag was the prettiest handbag I had ever seen, with beaded handles, all decorated with flowers.

'Wow. A real Gucci bag,' Chloe sighed.

'Sure is,' Maddy agreed, nodding. 'Even *I* say that's cute. Anything inside?'

I unclasped it and pulled out a box. In it was a pot of the expensive seaweed cream that I had wanted so badly. And a note. I read it out.

Chère *Carrie,*

I hope that you like the presents. I know you do not have such things.

You say sorry to me many times for thinking it is me who cut the dress of Chloe. How could you think such a thing of me? Incredible! So I do not speak with you. And girls from my own school think this too. I do not speak with them.

Then your mother came to talk with me for a long time. I tell her many things (but not about the night with Wayne Brennan). I tell her how I feel so bad that people could feel this way about me. She say money and clothes are very nice to have (which I know – naturellement*!) but perhaps to consider what I may have done for this to happen. She helps me think hard and now maybe now I see I did a few things to 'make you feel less than positive about me'. (Your mother told me this expression.) For this I am sorry and I give you the presents. I can tell you that I feel very positive about your mother – even though she think orange kaftan go nice with purple culottes and trainers. This makes me feel that I have learned some important things in my stay here.*

I learn I know more about designer labels than your friend Chloe, but that some people think she has more talent than me. Of course everyone is allowed their own opinion.

I learn not to think being in a band make you a special or nice person. Maybe very famous rock stars are different? Though I did not meet any of those on my visit. When I do, I will let you know.

I learn that if you do not live in a big city or near anywhere exciting that you can still have fun and be happy in a tiny, boring small place.

*I learn that though I could not believe I would ever think this,
you have many things I wish I had.*

I learn I cannot buy them.

Kisses,

Marie-Camille.

*P.S. I hope you like the bag. I give you the cream because I see
now that your spot has gone. This is good. You do not want Jack
to see it. He is good boyfriend. Cécile like him, she try to kiss him
but he say no, he likes only you.*

'*No way!* Cécile *did* try it on with him then?' Rani gasped.

'She did. Jack told me. He rang my mobile just after the coach
had gone.' I grinned.

'Why didn't he say anything before?'

'He said he thought Anglo-French relationships were
fragile enough and he didn't want to risk an international incident.'

'Probably wise, Carrie. You know what you're like.'

'Rani! Blimmin' cheek!'

'The main thing is that Marie-Camille very *nearly* looks like she
might have gained *something* by leaving the glamour of Paris and
coming here.'

'Almost. Did you know I was sort of impressed by all that stuff
when she first arrived?'

'Were you, Carrie? Surely not.'

'Shut up, Rani. I think I was dazzled by her being such a Paris
Princess. I was even a bit ashamed of my mum.'

'Who seems to have understood a lot more about Marie-
Camille than we did,' Chloe added. 'But don't be so negative, lots
of good stuff came out of the visit.'

'Lucy Kell appreciating what a star you are,' I went on. 'And Maddy's fantastic photographs, which are going to make such a brilliant display. I hear the local paper is interested in publishing some shots.'

'And my dad telling me he thinks I'm perfect just as I am and that he couldn't be more proud of me. Fare ye well, maths mentalists! Yee-ha!' announced Rani.

Chloe grinned. 'And making new friends. And realising that it's so lame to make judgements about people based on what they wear. Pop-socks rule!'

'And knowing money can't buy you love,' I shouted.

Rani had put on a pair of my shoes. She staggered on to my chair and clicked her heels together. 'There's no place like home! There's no place like home!' she cried.

'And I'm sure you must have all learned loads of French!' Maddy continued wildly.

We all turned to look at her and then burst out laughing.

Honestly. That girl has the best sense of humour.

 EVERYONE'S TIP • • • • • • • • • • • • • • •

Do something nice for someone else: it won't make your legs longer or your eyelashes curlier. But it will always make you beautiful. Every time.

Carrie and her friends, Rani and Chloe, each have a talent
for style – Carrie is great at design, Rani is gifted with make-up,
and Chloe has a flair for fashion. They're a great team – but
Carrie realises she has been neglecting Rani and Chloe in favour
of a boy. So she's decided to make an effort to be a better
person – which includes helping others to find the best in
themselves, as well as finding them the loves of their lives.
However, when her plans collide with reality, she realises
there are lessons to be had, as well as laughs.

Carrie knows that fashions change but style stays with you
forever. But which is true when it comes to friends?

The first book in the Style Sisters series.

Style Sisters

GREEN GODDESSES

Until now, Carrie's main contribution to saving the
planet has been the generous flow of magazines she
collects for recycling, and a vague feeling that more than
three electrical hair styling appliances may be excessive.
All this is about to change when their geography teacher
is replaced by the Byronic eco-warrior, Guy 'River' Trent.
With his idealistic views and high principles, not to
mention his long dark hair and rugged sweaters, he
soon has the whole year in an eco-frenzy.

Competition for his approval reaches a peak on the
Year Nine geography field trip to the Lake District.
As if that wasn't enough, life is made even harder by
the disgruntled boys on the expedition using
the school video camera to make *Boughton High:
Night of Terror* – with the Style Sisters starring . . .

The third book in the Style Sisters series.
Coming May 2007.

www.piccadillypress.co.uk

☆ The latest news on forthcoming books

☆ Chapter previews

☆ Author biographies

☆ Fun quizzes

☆ Reader reviews

☆ Competitions and fab prizes

☆ Book features and cool downloads

☆ And much, much more . . .

Log on and check it out!

Piccadilly Press